Nede Land 2: © 2020 by Dr. Yeral E. Ogando
The Hero Within – Nede Land 2
Publisher: Christian Translation LLC
Printed in the USA

This is a work of fiction. Names, characters, dialogue, places, and incidents are either a product of the author's imagination and are used fictitiously. Character's opinions are not necessarily the same as the authors. Any resemblance to persons living or dead is purely coincidental; they are not to be interpreted as real people or events.

ISBN 13: 978-1-946249-20-3

1. Series Fiction 2. Spiritual Warfare 3. Christian Fiction.

DEDICATION

This book is dedicated to the Unique and forever-lasting person who has always been there for me, no matter how stubborn I am:

GOD

I also want to dedicate this work to YOU (Rey Luis and Seferina), my beloved grandparents because without you, I would not been here. May you rest in peace with our Lord Jesus Christ in heaven! You were and will always be the best part of me.

I WILL ALWAYS LOVE YOU.

Always.

ACKNOWLEDGMENTS

Thanks to God for allowing my dream to come true, and for giving me strength when I felt like giving up.

Had it not been for the support that I have received along the way from these incredible and amazing people, I would not be where I am today.

Thanks to my editor, Lucas Walsh for doing such a great job helping me polish this book.

And I can't forget to mention Hiraida Diaz for her continuous support and brilliant ideas of The Hero Within series.

This has been a very long ride for my family, but the reward is worthy. Thanks to my daughters, Yeiris & Tiffany, my sons Bennett, Ethan and Nathan for staying by my side through this journey. You know I love you.

Chapter 1

Moon Ville

"We have gained knowledge and understanding about this new spiritual kingdom. When will the door be opened? I am eager to start this quest." Said Marvel, in a tone that betrayed a touch of desperation.

"Let us relax, pray, fast, and read the Word of God to feed our souls and ready ourselves for the next challenge. We know that whatever awaits us, it will not be easy. Let us remember that, if the Guardian is even half as violent as the people have told us, we are in for the fight of our lives." Added Psychic.

"Do you think we should gather tomorrow for a BPF?" She continued.

"Are you talking about what I *think* you're talking about?" Asked Marvel.

"Yes, I am. I am talking about *Bible, Praying and Fasting.*" Confirmed Psychic.

"Ok, I just wanted to make sure we are on the same page. Six a.m. sound good?"

"Excellent, we'll meet tomorrow then."

The next day at six in the morning exactly, when the sun was gently skirting the horizon at the edge of the world, projecting slender silver threads of light across the emerging blue mantle of dawn, both Marvel and Psychic were in BPF mode, as they call it. Several hours passed and, in the middle of an interception, they heard something far off in the distance.

"Marvel, can you hear that?"

"I don't hear anything." Whispered Marvel.

"What are you talking about? You can't hear that sound?" Asked Psychic incredulously.

"Pay attention!" She hissed. "I can hear bells ringing…like church bells."

"But we don't have bells in this city." Replied Marvel in confusion.

In that same moment of confusion and disbelief, God opened their eyes to the splendor of the spiritual kingdom, allowing them to see everything they needed to see.

Noom Live Kingdom

This is a kingdom of incredulous people, who believe only in their own consciences; if they don't have physical proof of something, they do not believe it exists. Some call them "scientists" because they deny anything that they cannot prove. They are well-educated and fine people.

Knowledgeable in all types of disciplines and wise, they are able to plan and scheme in ways that few can imagine, using their knowledge and resources to achieve unparalleled heights. They are always experimenting and testing to prove a theory or develop some new technology. They are called the *Scitpeks*.

The citizens of Noom Live Kingdom can be very polite, but also frightening and explosive with others of lesser knowledge or lesser understanding. A super intelligent people, their kingdom is modern, with buildings, factories, stores, supermarkets, and labs on every street. Valued above all, however, are the research facilities. In this kingdom, there is a pure and mighty river, called *Hogin River*. It is always clean and free of pollution as well, because it is the main source of seafood for Nede Land.

There is a legend that mentions a ruthless yet kind King. In one of his battles, he created the perfect strategy for defeating his enemies, and he sacrificed sixty percent of his troops to develop and perfect the strategy. King Suicufnoc and his most trusted scholar, Needrab, were the masterminds of the greatest battle of all time. They say that they put the troops at great risk to create an opening on the battlefield, allowing them to infiltrate the enemy camp unnoticed.

When the challenging King thought that the battle was over, and that he'd won, Suicufnoc and Needrab revealed themselves in the middle of the enemy camp. In a flash they beheaded all the generals and their King, claiming victory for Suicufnoc.

They are a tall race, frightening to the eyes, their strength and power beyond comprehension. Their reputation grew more fearsome, and this attracted people of a similar stamp and temperament. Eventually, they created their own race of geniuses, frightening and violent. At first sight, though, they do not give the impression that they are violent at all. Their intelligence surpasses human abilities, and they portray themselves as friendly and docile people, when in fact they have a hidden agenda that they advance with all their actions. Once they set themselves to a purpose, or locate a target, they release their true nature. This makes the *Scitpeks* proud.

According to legend, Needrab and Suicufnoc were like one, inseparable and indivisible. Their wives were expecting children at the same time, and when the time came for them to deliver, Needrab's wife had a boy and Suicufnoc's wife had a girl. Secretly, the legend goes, the women came up with a plan to switch their children. They knew that Suicufnoc wanted, *and needed* a son as his heir. A girl would be a disappointment and could not inherit the kingdom

A few days after they were born, the girl developed a strange type of fever, and no one in the kingdom was able to find a cure. On the evening when the sickness was at its worst, both wives were expecting their husbands at the same place with their children.

When their husbands arrived, they were told about the sudden fever. They despaired for their science and knowledge could not find the cure for the child. Needrab was devastated. He became despondent, and wrought up. He did not eat or leave his bed for days, certain that his daughter would die. His cries were unbearable and his pain otherworldly. For years they'd tried to conceive, and it was thought that their wives were barren. But Needrab and Suicufnoc developed a secret elixir to heal them, and they eventually conceived. Now, after all that, telling Needrab that the child could die was something he could not bear.

The affliction and pain in Needrab's heart was too much to bear, so his wife decided to share with him the secret, but not before making him promise never to divulge what she was about the tell him. She made him swear a blood pact that day. When she told him all the details behind the plot, Needrab was speechless.

He felt something warm and peaceful in his chest after he contemplated the information. He was relieved and they decided to continue with their lives. A few days later, Needrab and Suicufnoc were able to create another elixir for the girl and she recovered her health. The King praised Needrab for his diligence and perseverance in creating the elixir. After this, Needrab returned to his duties and as a token of appreciation, King Suicufnoc appointed Needrab as the tutor, teacher and Guardian of his son, the heir to the throne.

Needrab's daughter grew to be a strong, gorgeous woman, and a cunning fighter. Training alongside King Suicufnoc's son, who was himself known as a powerful, frightening and violent fighter, they both learned the tactics and style of Needrab. The King taught all the knowledge he had to his son. The King did not know that his son was sharing his training and knowledge with his best friend's daughter.

Now that they are grown, they always fight together. Needrab's daughter is the war strategist and the intelligence behind every battle, and Suicufnoc's son is the muscle, the brute force. Together they are like dynamite, explosive and violent and completely unstoppable; adversaries that you would never want to face. The girl's name is Pat and the boy's name is Jack.

Together, they founded a training academy, and it teaches skills that go beyond mere fighting. Needrab instructs all his pupils in strategy and tactical techniques, and they only accept new recruits that spend a full day with Pat and Jack. If the potential recruit does not pass Pat and Jack's assessment, they are deemed unworthy of entering the academy and do not receive knowledge from Needrab of Noom Live Kingdom. The academy is mainly focused on creating the best leaders and fighters in all the kingdom, with the ultimate purpose of creating the perfect candidate to participate in the yearly tournament, which is celebrated in Hont Well Kingdom. To join Hont Well Kingdom's tournament, fighters need to face Pat and Jack; only then they decide who can enter the tournament.

On the day of the battle, Needrab and the King realized that they needed to come up with a strategy that would ensure their survival, for if they did not, their fate would surely be sealed.

"This battle is fierce, and we cannot win it with brute force alone; we need to use our brains. After all, that's why we have them." Suicufnoc said with a cocked eyebrow. "Our numbers are few compared to theirs, and, at first glance, this is a lost cause. But," he said sneakily, "we have something they don't have."

"Of course, my friend! Their first mistake was trusting in their numbers, and their second mistake was belittling our numbers, and underestimating our capability." Agreed Needrab. "So how do we use that to our advantage? Our forces are few, and for us to pull this out, we will need to sacrifice most of our fellow comrades."

Chapter 2

"I am not inclined to that strategy, but it looks like we don't have another option." Sighed Suicufnoc gravely.

He stood up, and with resolution, delivered a few words of inspiration. "This is our moment to gain a fearsome reputation; to become something truly *great.* It will all depend on whether we are victorious here. If we are defeated, we shall never rise again. Let us rise! Rise and march defiantly into the crush of battle and draw one last glorious breath bedside each other!"

There was a great tumult and cheer among the soldiers encamped around Suicufnoc, who seemed to draw strength from his words.

"I don't want to die; it is not my time yet. *I* will choose the time and place for my death." Added Needrab with certainty.

Turning to face the assembly of soldiers, Suicufnoc drew a deep breath and bellowed a resounding message.

"The time has come for us to shape our future, and win this battle!" The men shouted gutturally in return, and clashed their swords and spears against their shields in unison. "It is always best to sacrifice the few for the sake of many, and today we are called upon to make this sacrifice! Are you with me!?" The men returned a battle cry of such force and tenacity, that all the soldiers of the opposing force could hear from across the field.

"So be it." Smiled Suicufnoc, turning toward the battle front, slamming the visor of his helmet down, his eyes gleaming with anticipation and fury.

. . . .

Suicufnoc whirled around and retreated into his command tent, beckoning Needrab to follow. Once inside, they surveyed the maps spread out before them, and sat to discuss their strategy.

"Let us select the most trusted soldiers for our final strike. By my calculations, we will need to sacrifice sixty percent of our troops to even have a hope of gaining victory and honor this day."

Needrab nodded in cold agreement. "Let us select the finest warriors we have to lead this attack." He said to Suicufnoc.

Suicufnoc looked across the tent to his general. "Gather the troops." He commanded.

After gathering the most trusted soldiers, both King Suicufnoc and his closest friend and general, Needrab, were able to come up with a grand strategy. Only the newly chosen men from his troop knew of the plan and how to carry it out.

"Needrab, send our final instructions to the front lines."

. . . .

The enemy trusted in their numbers, and were not afraid. They were ready to wipe the field of these *parasites*. It was getting dark, and the enemy was busy gathering firewood and provisions for the long night before the dawn, and their glorious victory. They were not aware there was a spy among them, who informed Needrab and Suicufnoc of all their movements.

The spy knew of the nightly routine of gathering supplies from the rear front, which faced the forest. These supply gathering groups would not normally be well equipped or prepared to fight. These facts were relayed to Suicufnoc's *chosen few, who overtook one of these groups of gatherers, slaughtered them, and assumed their identities.* Then, in disguise, they infiltrated the enemy's rear rank. Among them, were King Suicufnoc and General Needrab themselves. They positioned themselves throughout the ranks, surrounding the enemy with covert soldiers.

The enemy troop and their leader had a great feast that night, arrogant and overconfident, completely unaware of their enemy's plan. They feasted and drank and made merry; not falling asleep until the small hours of the morning.

. . . .

"Wake up! Wake up, my king! We are being attacked!" Shouted the guard.

"Attacked? By whom?" The king hurriedly rolled out of bed, still in his dressing gown, thinking his guard was being a complete moron. "The enemy is few, and we are well fortified. They could not have flanked us. What could possibly..."

He had not even finished his sentence, when out of nowhere came a voice, saying,

"Your time is over, weak and feeble king."

The king wheeled around to see his guard, gurgling blood from his mouth, collapse to the ground, his head rolling away from his body, revealing a menacing figure behind him.

"It is *my* time to shine." The mighty warrior, ready for the kill, struck fear into the king's icy heart. He tried to draw his own sword, but he felt a burning sensation in the back of his neck. He dared not turn, but he knew there was another at his back. It was Needrab. "How... how... how could this happen?" He stammered feebly. He opened his mouth to try and beg for mercy, but where words would have been, there was only the caustic metallic taste of his own blood. The king was dead before his knees hit the floor of his opulent tent.

His troops thinking they were driving the enemy back, began to realize that, though they had killed many of the enemy troops, their king and all their generals had been slaughtered right under their noses. As it dawned on the men, they quickly surrendered, utterly demoralized. But King Suicufnoc and Needrab annihilated almost every one of them, to solidify their victory, and crush the spirit of the country from which they had come. Those left alive were a reminder for his great victory, and on that day, Suicufnoc was crowned King of Noom Live Kingdom.

This legendary battle, immortalized in song and story throughout the kingdom, was won with strategy, spirit, and sharp eyes. Though it cost many lives, it marked the beginning of a new era for the new kingdom. Legend tells that to this day, not even the King understands exactly how they won.

Only a few soldiers know the true power of their king's sharp mind, or the unsurpassed might of his general. After the great battle, the newly named King Suicufnoc and the General of the Royal Guard, Needrab became as one; best friends and accomplices in all things.

....

"I am pleased with my kingdom, and with what we have accomplished together. Hogin River is cleaner than ever, and we are producing the best sea fish in all Nede Land. Commerce is excellent, but I think it is time for us to start a family. I don't want to be a king without a queen."

"Well, my King, I have been contemplating my future as well, and I, too, wish to sire children and take a wife." Reflected Needrab.

The King, pleased to hear this from his loyal friend, slapped Needrab's shoulder and laughed heartily. "Good! This celebration is the perfect opportunity for us to find the perfect women."

"You mean, to make the search public?" Needrab asked.

"Yes! Why not?"

Needrab pondered for a moment. "What about those twin sisters that are always flirting with us?" He offered.

"You are right. You know, Ynnafit has stolen my heart, and I know you are bewitched by her sister. Added King Suicufnoc with a smile and a nudge.

"Speaking of the devil!" There they are, making their big entrance to the celebration!" The King exclaimed, looking out the window into the courtyard below.

Needrab went to the window and looked as though he might fall over, right into the crowd.

"I think I feel weak, and my heart is beating too fast. I feel butterflies in my stomach. I am nervous." Needrab looked like he was on the verge of a panic attack.

"Hahaha!" The King laughed mightily. "Relax, my friend!" He put his arm around Needrab's shoulder. "Take a deep breath. It only means that you are feeling what I am feeling. This is called "love" and none of that "first-sight" business; this is real love."

. . . .

Meanwhile, in the courtyard, one of the sisters had noticed this spectacle taking place high above them.

"You need to dissimulate, sister. I think our heroes are looking at us. Don't stare! They'll feel more eager to come to us if you don't look. That is the way to gain man and keep him interested." Explained Siriey.

Siriey was a stunningly beautiful and charming young girl, and the oldest by a few minutes. She could enchant any man by simply opening her mouth to speak. Eloquent and intelligent, though not entirely or at all times aware of just how intelligent, Siriey was a miraculous woman. Of course, she was also a little erratic and, when overcome with emotions, she was prone to acting rashly, giving herself completely to a situation without a thought for the consequences.

Ynnafit on the other hand, was calm, calculating, and, some say, the brains of the two. People only needed to look at her to fall captive to her charms. Slim in body, with dark skin, much like Pocahontas, some even called her the Queen in their gossip circles.

Chapter 3

"Ladies and gentlemen, tonight we are witness to history! Our beloved King and his right hand will choose wives to accompany them, and to be by their sides forever!" The announcer lifted his voice so that all could hear him.

A voice of jest from the crowd said, "It will be a great loss for our brothels!" They all laughed while the speaker was giving the announcement and joking around. It was a night for celebration, anything was possible, and forgiven on this very special occasion.

There were many candidates, but none of them appeared to be worthy to be the future Queen and the future wife for the General.

But, when the twin sisters stood up, they were able to claim their rightful place after providing correct answers to the *challenge*.

Prior to the celebration, both King Suicufnoc and General Needrab had come up with a brilliant plan for seducing their wives. Only smart and cunning women could know the answers to their questions, which, after all, was a secret known to very few.

By providing correct answers, the twins proved to be worthy and capable, which had been the plan all along. The twin sisters finally had their hands on the men of their dreams.

....

"It is time for the King to announce the name or names of the candidates. If there is to be more than one for either of the bachelors, there must be an additional test to determine the winner."

King Suicufnoc announced that Ynnafit was his sole candidate. General Needrab announced that Siriey was to be his bride and future wife.

All in the kingdom shouted at once, "Long life to the twin sisters!" and "Long life to our King and First General!"

They celebrated love and happiness the entire evening. The King had finally found his future Queen and Ynnafit had finally found the love of her life.

There was no jealousy between the twin sisters; their hearts had been stolen a long time ago and they would now be able to tell the legends to their children and grandchildren of how they came to know their husbands.

....

After some years of happiness, it became apparent to the people of the kingdom that not all was well in the King's household. The citizens were anxious that they should have an heir to their beloved kingdom, yet, no heir had yet been produced. Soon rumors spread that the twins could not conceive, and there was great unrest among the people. King Suicufnoc and Needrab devised a miraculous cure for this infertility in their secret laboratory. They were anxious to have their own children and to create a lasting dynasty. They felt powerless, but using their intelligence and science, they created the tool they needed for conceiving. They did not pray to God or the gods, they did not believe in any of these ancient stories, as they called them.

They could only believe what their eyes told them, and science showed them. What they could not prove to be right by testing, was nothing to them. After all, they were the heads of the *Scitpeks Group*, who believe only in science, and not in the gods of their forefathers or the only true God.

After several attempts with the formula, it was in the fifth year of King Suicufnoc and General Needrab's reign that their wives conceived. They could not have been happier; after all the struggles, they were finally going to have their offspring.

Even in times of peace, a rival group would occasionally arise to challenge King Suicufnoc and conquer the kingdom. The King and his family were resting and living happily when they heard about a threat to the kingdom, they set to foot and got ready for battle, leaving their wives with a mere two months to give birth. They promised to be back in a few days, but little did they know that they were not going to be by their wives' sides at the moment of giving birth. While the two men were still in battle, the twin sisters gave birth. A boy to one sister, and a girl to the other.

....

Pat and Jack were like brother and sister. As they grew up and fought in many battles, so grew their reputations. They even made nick names for themselves. Pat was known as the Python, and Jack, the Panther. The perfect duo could annihilate any rival or enemy in no time. Yet, neither one of them was aware of the true meaning behind their names. As far as they knew, they were living up to the reputation of their kingdom, and of their fathers.

....

"My King, I hate to bring bad news, but the gate from earth has been opened and I fear we may have a war approaching." Said Needrab.

"But you are the Guardian of that gate, and I don't know anyone who would be strong enough to defeat you." Replied King Suicufnoc, dismissively.

"My King, you are correct, I *am* the Guardian. But..." Needrab struggled. "I have been defeated by two vicious and evil opponents, and I believe they will soon head to the kingdom...for war.

The King stood in complete shock, grasping Needrab by the arm in concern.

"But how are you alive?" He exclaimed.

"Well, the requirement to open the gate was to find a worthy opponent, strong enough to defeat me, and I fear I have found two instead of one."

"Did it occur to you that I do not *want* anyone coming to my kingdom? That is why, I appointed you, my friend, as the Guardian. Because you were the only one I could count on." The King said bitterly, as though he felt betrayed.

"My king, I am still here." Replied Needrab resolutely.

"Yes, you are here, but intruders are coming to my kingdom and you have granted them safe passage. I will need to think about your treachery seriously after we overcome this situation together."

"My King, why not let the young Prince handle this threat? I am sure he will be able to defeat them. After all, they have surpassed even our skills and abilities." Suggested Needrab.

"As I said before, we will look together for a way to overcome this without involving our children. I am sure that if the Prince is going to fight, your daughter will fight too. Don't you fear for their lives?" Inquired the King.

"I do, my king, but they have surpassed our expectations and grown stronger than anyone in the kingdom.

A dark secret was engulfing Needrab's heart which he will not reveal anytime soon.

. . . .

"Nevertheless, I knew this day would come, so I have prepared a backup measure for anyone coming to my kingdom uninvited." Added King Suicufnoc. "Whoever they are, they will only be able to step *into* my kingdom, but nothing further."

"I was not aware of any second measure, my king. Somehow you forgot to mention it to me." Added Needrab with a tinge of anger. "May I know the nature of this *extra measure* you've taken?"

"Don't worry about it!" Shouted the King, still angered with Needrab. "You will see it first-hand. Have you forgotten, my friend, that we always foresee what is to come and we take measures long in advance, to get the results we want? Why do you think we have all these labs, spread throughout the kingdom?" Continued saying the King. "Did you think it was *purely* for medical research? You were involved in some of the labs, the ones dedicated to science and birth giving; That is how we came up with our children. But I was involved in something more than that. I must ensure the peace of my kingdom at all costs."

"So, all this time, you did not trust my judgment or strength?" Asked Needrab, hurt beyond measure.

"On the contrary, my dear friend; I have always had, and will always have full confidence in you and your strengths. These were only precautions. I never thought of using them, or that someone might defeat you someday, but as you know, we must be prepared at all times. But enough about that. In fact, I am glad that we are having guests in the kingdom, even if they are *uninvited* guests. It gives me the perfect opportunity to test our true abilities and strength. We will see how good our scientific development team really is. Come, my friend, let us sit down and enjoy the show. As you can see, I have eyes all over the kingdom and anything that moves will be detected by my security system."

Chapter 4

Suddenly, there was a strange sound, like a bell, but Needrab had never heard it before. "What is that sound I hear?"

"That, my friend, is the signal that we have company. Intruders are in our kingdom."

"I will go immediately and stop them!" Shouted Needrab.

"Haven't you been listening? There is no need for that, my friend." Said the King, dismissively. "There is a team already in place waiting for our uninvited guests. It seems like we have two guests. What should we do? Should we clear the path for them, or should we just stop them where they are and avoid the trouble?" Inquired the King, slyly.

"Well, my King…" Said Needrab, taking his seat uselessly.

"It was not a question!" Interrupted the King abruptly. "I was just having fun with you and getting some excitement out of it. It has been a long time since we had some fighting, or any challenges at all. If they have defeated you, then, they are the challenge I have been waiting for."

"Let us walk, you and I, to *the cage*." Said King Suicufnoc.

"The cage...?" Replied Needrab, surprised by this statement. "I did not even know we had a...cage."

"Yes, we do. But this one is designed especially for uninvited guests. We will find them there, of course. That is, *if* we hurry. I fear that my Cage Unit or Dungeon Unit might have too much fun fighting them and may kill them before I have the time to talk to them. C'mon, let us hurry!"

"Dungeon Unit, Cage Unit...?" Wondered Needrab.

. . . .

"We have trapped two birds in the cage!" Laughed one of the soldiers in the dungeon area. "We should hurry up and have some fun before the King arrives."

. . . .

"I am confused. We just stepped into this kingdom and we are already trapped. We need to find a way out of this immediately." Said Psychic.

"Yes, you are right. We did not come to this kingdom to be imprisoned or to be in a cage." Added Marvel. "We must fight our way out."

Marvel and Psychic were not aware that their words would be literally true, and that they would have to fight for survival.

....

Marvel and Psychic had a little knowledge of how this new spiritual world works, but they did not know the extent of it. Lord, we did not come to be trapped!

....

"Welcome to the cage!" Shouted a group of soldiers, cheering and hollering into the pit.

"It looks like we're having fun today, boys! Two birds have come to play." Yelled the head of the Dungeon Guard, with a wicked smile. He was the one they called "Zero", and the more than 20 guards positioned around the cage began cheering his name.

"Calm down guys, we gotta place bets! Should we allow them to fight together, or one on one?" Zero asked the crowd.

Raising his head, Marvel calmly said, "Why don't all of you come down here and fight us at once? The soldiers laughed uproariously in disbelieve.

They could not believe their ears. Did this young boy, who looked no more than twenty five years old, really think he could fight them all at once?

"Let us call this one…" Zero, pointing to Marvel, "…the *freckle boy*. Yeah, that's good. And the woman," he stared at Psychic, "we will call her *the guest*."

Psychic, who had been sitting in the dirt until this point, stood up and said,

"Thank you for your generosity, but we already have names. He's Marvel," She cocked her head in Marvel's direction confidently, "and I am Psychic. But that's already more than you deserve to know. Now! Let's get this rolling, and be done with it. We don't have time to waste with weaklings like you."

Suddenly things weren't so funny anymore. The guards started tightening their armor and drawing their swords and knives, getting ready to jump into the cage.

"Send in the first group of losers!" Shouted Marvel.

"Well, well, you are eager to die." Laughed Zero. "So be it. The first guards you'll be fighting are *ZeroOne*, *ZeroNine*, *ZeroSix* and *ZeroEighteen*."

When Psychic and Marvel heard their names, they started bellowing with laughter. "You don't even have real names!" Wheezed Marvel.

"You are all *zeroes*! Hahaha! If I moved you all to the left, would you be valueless?" Psychic and Marvel could not control themselves.

"Your master must have no love for you at all, or you must have no value yourselves. *Zeroes.*" Marvel burst into laughter again, infuriating the guards.

. . . .

Zero Six and Zero Eighteen stepped into the cage. The cage was octagonal, approximately 750 square feet, 30 feet across and 6 feet high, and it had been created with fighting in mind. Its walls and padded surfaces protected fighters from falling or getting thrown out. It was completely closed off except for one door that could only be opened from the outside.

On top of that, there were extra security layers in the walls; bars and fence with razor wire coiled around the top, thus making it impossible to escape. It looked like the perfect arena for fighting a championship.

"The rules are simple; fight your way out of the cage. If you manage to defeat our four main fighters, we will not only allow you to live, we will escort you to the King ourselves. Lose, and you'll die. There are no restrictions on combat, anything goes. It is a fight to the death. If you tap out, signaling defeat, we will throw you into the electrical chamber." Zero concluded with this and the men chuckled around him in anticipation, as if it was a favored pastime.

"If you don't tap before you are defeated, you will still die, but because more fighters will enter the cage. The fighters have clear instructions on killing you. Make no mistake, this is a fight to the death."

"What if we defeat your fighters and they don't get the chance to tap?" Asked Marvel.

"Ha! If that happens, you are free to kill him! If the next one after that taps, then the next one will enter the cage. Only by defeating our four fighters can you escape. Each one of you will fight two of our fighters, one at a time. You must win each of the matches to get out of the cage, and for every fight you lose, another two fighters will enter the cage."

. . . .

"I hear some commotion among the guards. Mentioned Python. "I don't know what's going on, but it looks like we may have some fun here soon." He rose from where he was lounging, and Panther responded, "It is about time. Let us go see what is happening."

"It has something to do with the Secret Entrance to the kingdom, I'll wager. My father showed me the path to the gate a long time ago. It's just beyond an underground encampment." Panther mused while they walked along at a healthy pace.

"Are you talking about that *cage* thing we used to play in when we were young?" Added Python.

"Exactly! C'mon!" He broke out into a run, beckoning Python to follow.

As they ran, side by side, Panther started a conversion.

"Do you remember how much fun we had at that place?"

"How could I forget? You knocked me right through one of those rickety walls the first day. You've never known your own strength, *your highness.*" Replied Python with a gleam.

"Ha! I don't remember that! Are you sure that was the first day?" They both leapt over a hill and landed hard, creating a dust cloud.

"Oh, I see. You remember almost killing me, but you don't remember when? That's rich."

"Maybe my memory isn't as good as it once was because you've slammed my head into the ground too many times!"

Their pace was incredible, creating a blur in the air as they ran. In no time at all, they arrived at the entrance. Panther strode over to a small gap in the shrubbery of the underbrush, where there seemed to be a collapsed stone wall. He passed his hand over a mound of moss, and the stones silently separated from one another, rolling out of the way and exposing a small entrance leading to a tunnel.

He gestured to Python to enter.

"It's kind of dark in here, but I know the path." Reassured Panther.

As they travelled through the tunnel, it opened up into another road just a few hundred yards beyond the entrance. Turning around a bend in this path rather hastily, they bumped into two men walking the same way.

When these two strangers turned around to see who had accosted them, Panther and Python immediately came to attention.

"Father." Said Panther, shocked and embarrassed.

"What are you two doing here and where do you think you are going? This is not a place for you two to be. Turn back and continue with whatever you were doing, we will handle this ourselves." Scolded King Suicufnoc with an angry tone of voice. Both Panther and Python were surprised at his tone of voice.

"As you command, your majesty." The two said in unison, stepping back a few paces then turning to retreat along the path.

When they'd walked far enough back down the path, out of earshot of the King and the General, Python turned to Panther and said,

"Something that our fathers don't want us to see is going on, something weird."

"Well, I thought this place was just an abandoned spot in the kingdom, one that I happened to know how to access where we could keep a lookout if we wanted. Let's go back and find out." Said Panther.

Surprised, Python responded, "Hey, you know I've got your back, but are you sure you want to disobey the King's command?"

"Don't worry, nobody will know. Besides, if you're right, they're too old for this stuff." Panther grinned.

Chapter 5

"I'll tell you what we are going to do," Said Marvel in a very impatient tone of voice, "I will fight your four zeroes..." and he snickered, trying to control himself. "Psychic, please sit down and enjoy the show."

Only two of them entered the cage; ZeroOne and ZeroSix. ZeroOne possessed no hesitation, and as soon as his feet hit the dirt, he cocked back his fist to strike Psychic. But he barely extended his arm before he was hurled against the wall of the cage with a thunderous blow from Marvel.

"I did say, didn't I? You'll all be fighting me!" ZeroOne was regaining his composure and lifting himself from the floor. "If either of you expect to last three minutes, you'll have to attack me together." Yelled Marvel with anger and ferocity.

Psychic just smiled. She didn't even blink when Marvel landed that flying kick on ZeroOne; she knew they were no match for him...or her.

ZeroOne and ZeroSix both rushed Marvel predictably.

"Is this what you wanted, you arrogant bastard!" Shouted ZeroSix amid a blinding flurry of kicks and punches. It appeared to them as though Marvel was stunned, taking the blows one right after another without even resisting. Blood was spattering across the walls and soaking into the dirt. They had him. But they were slowing down from the effort it took to wail on him. So they paused for a moment, completely exhausted.

"Had ENOUGH?" Huffed ZeroOne between gasps.

Marvel looked like a bloody marionette, standing as though he were loosely suspended from wires, about to keel over. But what they didn't know, was that Marvel wasn't hurt, he wasn't even phased.

"You should surrender…before it's too late." Marvel's lips curled into a twisted grin of satisfaction.

ZeroSix replied, "It looks like you don't seem to understand the situation. You're a bloody mess! You haven't countered even one of our attacks. I think you're delusional, kid!" And they both tried to laugh even though they were out of breath.

"At least you're half right." Marvel shot back. "Half right but all stupid." The Zeroes stopped laughing. I haven't countered, you're right. But that doesn't mean I haven't landed my own attacks. Look at yourselves, boys."

ZeroOne and ZeroSix broke out into a cold sweat, and in terror looked down at themselves.

"That blood isn't mine, you absolute fools. It's yours."

"How…blerch…is it possible? We have been hitting him, he hasn't even tried to attack." Gurgled ZeroOne through a haze of pain and blood.

"Don't overthink it. Are you ready for a taste of my real power?"

Marvel seemed to vanish in a cloud of dust, appearing behind the two stupefied guards. He sunk a fist into each man's back like a sledgehammer. ZeroOne and ZeroSix's eyes rolled over in shock. They hit the floor and curled up, completely unconscious.

"I'm not going to kill them!" Yelled Marvel to Zero. "They lost; the fight is mine. As I said before, you may all enter the cage to fight us. *That* would be equal, more or less. But you'd still be at a disadvantage. I can't really help that though, you guys just suck."

Python and Panther had been watching the fight from a distance, and now they were anxious for their turn to fight these newcomers.

"They are really strong. Just what the doctor prescribed." Said Python, and they both laughed.

ZeroNine and ZeroEighteen entered the cage. These two had trained together for years, developing a dual kickboxing style. Now seemed like the perfect time to test some new moves. Both of them descended on Marvel with two spin kicks, one on each side of him. He blocked them both with ease. They let fly with the full fury of their kickboxing style, trying to finish the fight immediately. This was a completely ineffective strategy, and they noticed.

Without missing a beat, both ZeroNine and ZeroEighteen drew their swords and prepared for a new approach. But Marvel had no intention of letting them use weapons. He spun through the air with a flying axe kick, smashing both of them into the ground and winning the round.

King Suicufnoc and General Needrab had also been observing the strength displayed by these fighters, and decided to mix things up a bit. The King nodded to Zero, who then gave the signal to his men. A group of 10 guards dropped into the cage to challenge Marvel. Suicufnoc wanted to see for himself the power that apparently defeated his greatest General.

With no more effort than he'd exerted to defeat the previous two guards, Marvel flicked his wrist and spun around on his heel, delivering a shockwave punch and a whirlwind kick that devastated the entire group at once.

"That's it?" He whispered to himself.

Psychic hadn't moved from where she'd been sitting, and aside from dodging the odd unconscious minion whom Marvel had tossed her way by accident, she'd remained perfectly still.

Infuriated by her demeanor, Needrab ordered all of the remaining guards to pile into the cage. Psychic rolled her eyes.

"Are you serious? It took *this* long for you to throw out everything you've got? Pathetic."

Before even the first guard had touched the ground, Psychic drew her cutlass, and with a single blinding swing of the razor-sharp edge, she completely blew them all away like tumbling leaves in the wind.

There was a dead silence now. The dust had settled, and the defeated foes had stopped groaning. There were only three that remained outside the cage; King Suicufnoc, Needrab and Zero. Python and Panther were still concealed in their hidden spot.

"You are strong, I'll give you that." Said King Suicufnoc, seeing all his fighters on the ground unconscious. He snapped his fingers, and in the blink of an eye, a whole troop of fresh soldiers appeared around him as if from nothing.

"Treat the injured, and bring the intruders to me. We will see how strong they really are."

"I cannot believe my father called his personal guard into this. They are ruthless, trained assassins." Whispered Panther. The King's Guard were the most skilled assassins in all the land, and were

Suicufnoc's chosen competitors for the Soultai tournament.

"I for one am thrilled. It means we will get to fight them!" Said Python with a gleam in her eye.

. . . .

"Nice to see you, old man." Said Marvel, casually saluting Needrab. "Are we going to fight you for real this time?" But Needrab merely turned on his heel, without acknowledging them, and left. He didn't even ask the King's leave.

Marvel and Psychic allowed themselves to be brought before the King, but on the way up and out of the cage, Marvel turned to Psychic and whispered,

"Psychic, did you notice something strange back there?"

"What do you mean?"

"I could feel a pair of eyes looking at us from somewhere hidden. They were evil eyes and somehow they felt familiar to me."

"Yes, I noticed a presence that was familiar to me as well, but I don't know how to describe it exactly. Whoever they are, they are strong and savage." Added Psychic.

"In any case, it is apparent that the real battle has not started yet. We have the guardian, and I could sense a colossal power coming out of the one they call *The King*." Mused Marvel.

"We need to be careful with these people, there is something sinister about them, and nothing is as it seems. I believe they were only testing our skills. We cannot afford to be careless, we have a goal, after all. We need to find the Secret Treasures and retrieve them. According to the guard, they hold a terrible secret that does not belong to them. It belongs to humanity."

Chapter 6

"What do you want in my kingdom? What are you looking for? Asked King Suicufnoc with terrible seriousness. His cold command and searching gaze were magnetic. He was not to be trifled with.

"We came for the Secret Treasures your kingdom holds from humanity. We want them and we will get them by any means necessary." Stated Marvel plainly.

"The Secret Treasures? Do you even know anything about them? Do you have the faintest idea what they look like?" Mocked King Suicufnoc. "I will tell you what we will do. I will have you fight two of my Personal Guard. If you defeat them, you can have these relics of yours. Of course, you must also defeat the Guardians of the Treasures, but I cannot help that."

The King turned slightly to one of his men.

"Captain, call the best of your men who fought in the Soultai tournament and bring them here to fight these…intruders." He said the last word with scorn.

Zeroes came to the palace to defeat the two warriors who'd come from Earth. "How about that, there are two fighters with the same name." Thought Psychic.

"Fight them, and if you win, you will get your wish." Remarked the King dismissively.

The Zeroes were twin warriors, trained in the way of *Noom Live Kingdom*. They were two vicious, violent and irrational brothers. By looking at their eyes, you could tell they only wanted blood. They are not the type to think much, and they always go for the kill. That is why the king appointed them the head of the Dungeon Unit. Their strength and abilities are almost the same as the King's, or even better. They were selected long ago by Panther and Python. They proved their value and their strength a hundred times over. The twins have been trained in all types of fighting , and they've learned countless techniques, all of which they have mastered.

. . . .

Noom Live Kingdom was proud to be called the kingdom of *Meekness* and to have the best *interpreters of tongues* in *Nede Land*. Whenever an ancient text emerged that no one was able to understand, *Noom Live* People were the ones to call, with their technology and scientists.

At first glance, they look like regular people, unassuming and mild, but their knowledge and intellect is beyond compare.

. . . .

In all the battles they had fought throughout the years, never had they used their full strength. They hold back their true power and potential. Marvel and Psychic have not yet transformed into their Ultimate Forms.

"Do you think we will need our *secret technique* with these two?" Asked Psychic, leaning over to Marvel.

"Don't worry about it. Let's just play it cool until our goal is within reach. After all, our goal is not to fight, but to retrieve the holy relics and take them back to humanity." Said Marvel.

. . . .

The King summoned the two rivals to fight the intruders.

"After serious consideration, I think the Zeroes will win this battle with no problem." Remarked the king. "What do you think, Needrab?" Inquired the king.

"The intruders are very strong; I could sense their power when I was escorting them from the cage to the palace. We should be very careful with them. Maybe we should have other warriors fight them instead." Added Needrab.

"Nonsense! There is no way they will defeat the Zeroes, that is why I chose them. Get ready to signal the battle and start the fight." Commanded the King.

Needrab had a secret plan concealed in his heart and he was trying to reach the intruders.

"It is time for battle." Said Needrab. "I told you this was not a fight you can easily win. They are stronger than me." He released them into the arena to fight.

"Do not worry, old man. These are the not the ones who will defeat us." Reassured Psychic with a wink.

"Are you *Zeroes* going to fight fair? I guess I'll take the dark-skinned one, and you can take the blonde." Stated Marvel, sounding bored.

"There is but one rule. *Win at all costs*. Lose, and your souls will be mine forever." Said King Suicufnoc.

Both Marvel and Psychic thought to themselves,

"Our souls are already taken; they belong to our only *Lord* and *Master*. He is the one who sent us here, you lunatic king."

The Zeroes silently stepped forward, and, nodding at one another in perfect unison, they both blasted toward their targets with incredible speed, each landing a blow that could've moved a mountain, but they were blocked at the last second by Marvel and Psychic. After a few minutes of dodging and ducking, striking and blocking, the dark-skinned twin landed a blow on Marvel. This infuriated Psychic, who leapt off her feet and blazed the blonde twin with an ultimate attack from just the scabbard of her sword alone. The Zero was utterly defeated.

"I see." Said Needrab. The King, on the other hand, was speechless.

"She did not even use her sword. Who are you people?" Inquired the King.

"We've already told you what we want, that is more than enough for now." Responded Marvel while still fighting his opponent. The blond one, it seemed, was stronger, putting up more of a fight than his twin, who he did not seem to notice had been defeated. He even managed to legitimately hurt Marvel, compelling him to use his flying ax technique. This was enough to stop the twin in his tracks, where he fell over unconscious.

Marvel and Psychic felt the overwhelming presence again, and worry crept its way in to their minds for the first time since their arrival. At that is when Python and Panther showed themselves.

"This presence is stronger and more violent. The King and the Guardian do not compare to them. Who are they?" Marvel thought to himself.

When they turned, they saw for the first time the two warriors from the book, as if they had come to life. It was Pat the Python and Jack the Panther, alive and walking toward them.

"Why are they so strong? We've defeated them on earth, so what are they doing here?" Thought Psychic and Marvel, now connected in their thoughts. "This is not good, not good at all."

"Meet the guardians of the two holy relics you have been looking for." The King chuckled. "My son, Jack the Panther and Needrab's daughter, Pat the Python."

When Needrab heard these words, he was shocked. He was not aware that his own beloved daughter, and the King's son were the Guardians. "Things are not going according to my plan." Thought Needrab. "This is an unexpected outcome, but I cannot reveal what is buried deep in my heart. The secret that kept me going all these years."

"Wait!" Shouted Needrab. "I cannot allow these intruders to have access to our secret treasures. I will fight them once again, but this time, I will use all my strength to defeat them."

"Hold on! If I understand you correctly, you're saying that you lost on purpose?" Inquired King Suicufnoc in disbelief.

"No, my King, that is not what I said. What I mean is that I will make sure to defeat them even if it costs me my last breath." Needrab said with a grim bow.

"You of all people should know that I cannot back down on my word; they will have what they came for. Of course, they will need to fight Panther and Python to complete their mission." Everyone in the chamber starting laughing.

"Defeat Panther and Python? Poor creatures. You've come to look for something and you'll end up in the hands of the hunters. Panther and Python will be the end of you. Since I am a meek king, I will give you a few days to recover, and then we will celebrate the battle. I don't want you to think that we are being unfair, of course." The King said with a sneer of contempt.

"We'll fight you three days from now." Said Panther.

"Take them back to their cage; feed them and treat them to all the luxury we have to offer, and make sure they have everything they need to prepare the battle. After all, they'll be dead soon." Suicufnoc stated with conviction and spite. "Take them away."

Chapter 7

Psychic and Marvel were relatively unhurt from
their fight with the twins, just a few scratches on the
surface; but somehow, they felt like there was
something else going on behind the scenes.

"There is something fishy going on with the old
man." Said Marvel to Psychic. "I know he is strong,
and that he did not use his full strength when
fighting us. What's his angle, do you think? He gave
us intel on the kingdom and his words were true.
Why does he want us to succeed in our mission, and,
more importantly, why does it appear that he wants
to *stop* us now?"

They cleaned themselves in the facilities provided
them in the cage, and retired for the evening. They
could not help but wonder about the events of the
day and the many twisting turns it had taken. They
slept fitfully, tossing and turning with dreams of
what was to come.

On the second day, Marvel and Psychic had an
unexpected guest call at their cage. It was Needrab.

"I was wrong, you cannot win this battle. I will help
you escape, and you must promise you will return to

your homes and never attempt to come back here."
He said frantically.

"There is only one way for us to leave this kingdom,
and it is with the holy relics we came for. If you
hand them over to us, we will leave and vow never
to return. On the other hand, if you don't, we will
fight your daughter and she will definitely lose."
Retorted Psychic. "Not only will she lose miserably,
but so shall the King's precious son."

"They may be stronger than you, old man, but you
have not seen our power yet, and our mission is not
of this kingdom; it comes from the Most *High* and
we will not fail." Marvel added with conviction.

Needrab did not understand who they were talking
about, but he was committed to freeing them and
returning them to their homes before they fought
Panther and Python.

"You are too arrogant to see reason, but it will be as
you wish." He declared, relenting to the pressure of
the duo. As he turned to head back to the palace, he
stopped abruptly. "If I get you the holy relics, will
you leave and forfeit the fight?"

"Yes, we will." Said Marvel

"We don't want to fight, but we will if we must. Our
goal is to retrieve what was stolen from humanity
and restore the balance." Added Psychic.

"Very well then, I will do my best to get the holy relics." Needrab stated with a deep sigh. He knew it would not be easy, but it was his only hope.

Psychic and Marvel were not aware of many things concerning Needrab's revelation.

"He must be hiding something, that he would risk his kingdom and the wrath of his King." Marvel stated reflectively.

They did not know, but they were still praying for a glorious victory in their hearts.

. . . .

"Who is there? Show your face or you will regret it!" Said Python. "Come out immediately."

"It is I, your father." Answered Needrab.

"Ah, I am sorry, father. I did not know it was you. I sensed that someone was trying to steal my sword."

"You sensed correctly, Pat; I want your sword. I will hand it over to the intruders, and they will leave peacefully. Neither you nor Jack have to face them."

"Father, what are you talking about?" Python rose from her chair in disbelief. "Why is this sword so important? Why do you want me to concede defeat, when I know I can win?"

"Pat, up until now I was not aware that your sword possessed a hidden power. There are two holy relics in this kingdom, two *holy swords* representing two virtues of humanity. We cannot use the power in the sword, but humans can."

"You are saying that my sword is a holy sword. But if that is the case, why has the king given it to me?"

"Your sword holds the *Gift of Tongues*, that is why our kingdom is able to speak and decipher any and all languages. The power hidden within the sword grants all of us this power. I myself don't understand why the King has given it to you and not to his son. Maybe my son has the other holy sword."

"Your *son,* father…?" Python's eyes went wide with revelation.

"Please forgive me, sometimes I forget that he is not my son. I treat you both as my children."

"It is ok father, I know that." Said Pat. "However, I cannot give you the sword. I cannot violate the King's trust. I will fight. End of discussion."

Needrab knew that arguing with Pat was a lost cause, so he decided to pay a visit to the King's son, Jack.

. . . .

"Jack, are you awake?"

"Yes, Master, I am." Whispered the young Prince when he realized it was his faithful teacher.

"What are you doing here at this late hour?" Inquired Jack.

"I was trying to reason with Pat, but there is no reasoning with her. She is determined to fight and I want to avoid this particular battle at any cost." Said Needrab.

"But why…? Don't you have confidence in our skills? You have taught me so much and so has my father. They are not match for us. We will fight and win for sure."

"My son, I don't want to risk your life over a holy sword that does not belong to our kingdom."

"But there is no risk at all. Do not worry yourself, Master. We will win." Jack was growing confused and suspicious. "I don't understand what the big deal is about these swords anyway." He added.

"You don't understand, they are stolen virtues from humanity." Needrab pleaded. "Our kingdom is the guardian of two of these virtues. We have been hiding it from humanity, so that they don't take possession of these virtues themselves; there is no hope for them. The holy power in the swords can only be wielded by a human, while we only can see the reflection of the power. Even still, you and my daughter have been victorious in all your battles while you have been carrying them."

"You are saying that it is not because of our skills and techniques? It's because of the swords we carry." Said Jack, dismayed.

"Not exactly. But more or less. Let me hand the sword to them, thus avoiding the confrontation."

Jack the Panther became angry. Hearing that his master had so little faith in him made him feel bitter and distraught.

"Get out of my sight! We will FIGHT them, and we will win! We will prove to you that we have the power. They are no match for us. Now leave me alone!"

Chapter 8

"Our children will face these terrible foes, and they may very well lose. We cannot allow them to fight. We must stop this nonsense." Said Ynnafit to Siriey.

"But what can we do?" Siriey replied.

"We must speak to Needrab, and threaten him with revealing the truth. He'll have no choice but to stop the fight."

They both went immediately to seek out Needrab, to implore him, and to *threaten* him if necessary. They found him sitting with his head in his hands, looking extremely disappointed.

"Needrab! You have to stop this fight, our children cannot die! If you don't stop the fight, we will reveal the truth to the King!" Ynnafit shouted.

In a desperate and depressed tone. "I have no way to stop this fight. I have tried and the children will not listen to me. They are determined." He began to laugh morbidly. "You are free to try and speak with them yourselves!" His tone shifted drastically to one of displeasure. "But never again threaten me with revealing the truth. You asked me to vow with my own blood and I did."

Meanwhile, Jack was brooding in his room. He was pacing angrily and decided to go see Pat.

"I am so angry that Master does not trust in our skills!" Shouted Jack the Panther to Python.

"Yes, I feel equally frustrated at the moment. I feel like something inside of me is about to explode." Confirmed Pat. "I am about to burst."

At that moment, Ynnafit and Siriey showed up.

"We thought you'd be here. After all, you have been together since childhood. Why wouldn't you seek each other out for support? Listen, dear children, we don't want you to suffer and we want to stop this fight."

"You too mother!"

"Auntie! I cannot believe that the only one who trusts our skills is my father."

"You are misunderstanding the issue here." Soothed Ynnafit, approaching Panther and Python at the same time. "Your father is worried about you too. He does not want any harm to come to you; it is not that he does not trust you, it is simply that he does not want his children to get hurt."

"You've spoken to my father the King and he told you that? I cannot believe it!" Panther threw his hands in the air in frustration.

"There is a secret that we have been hiding from you all these years. *Needrab* is your father. He is the father of both of you."

"Of course, I know, he is like a father to me, not only my Master." Shouted Jack, blinded with rage.

"Just sit down and listen to us, because you still don't understand."

Jack and Pat relented reluctantly, and sat beside their mothers.

When they sat down, Ynnafit and Siriey shared with them the issues they went through when they were born; the disease and the swap.

"It means that I am not the rightful heir to the throne." Said Panther dismally. "It means that Pat is the rightful heir. Pat, this is what you always wanted. *You* are the true heir to the throne."

"The king is my father…" Pat the Python burst into tears. "The king is my father. I am of royal blood! The king is my father!" She was overwhelmed with joy. "Does my father know the truth?" She asked.

"No, he does not." Answered both mothers, simultaneously. "But he should not learn of this at least until we get ready to tell him. Please hand over the swords and stop the fight."

Each of them hugged their mothers, having realized that their true mother was in fact their aunt. It was a moment of tears and joy at the same time.

"Now, we are more convinced than ever that we can defeat the intruders in the name of the kingdom."

From this moment on, a new fire burned inside both Pat the Python and Jack the Panther. They both wanted to make their fathers proud. And they came up with a subtle way to send the message.

....

"I want the king to fight them instead," Thought Needrab, "I never intended for my son to fight these warriors. I know that if they fight the *king* they would probably win. I want to see the king defeated and my son on the throne as the rightful king. Only after that will I tell him the truth about his father. The king played his card without my consent, I was not aware they were the guardians of the treasures; I thought the king was the only guardian." How could he have done that to me? What does all this mean for his friendship with the King? All these things raced through the General's mind as he walked down the cobblestone path through the courtyard.

"The fight is inevitable. I will need to think of another plan."

....

It was the day of the fight, and the entire kingdom was present. They all wanted to enjoy the fight and the festivities, confident that the King would announce the victory of the kingdom with a sigh of relief and pride.

The King stepped up to the dais and strode across the carpeted floor to the gilt podium. The sea of people before him cheered and swelled like the ocean before the prow of a majestic ship. Suicufnoc stretched his mighty arms upward in a gesture of praise and confidence. His eyes gleamed as he stared into the foment of the whistling crowd, thinking back to the time when he was a lowly warrior vying for glory and reputation. These people had become his subjects all those years ago, and ever since that time he had dedicated his life to fostering their well-being and increasing their dignity. In that moment he felt the weight of those past decades bearing down on his conscience. "These children have come to rob me of my greatest treasure. Ha! They think they can take anything from *me?* Not now. Not ever."

He lowered his hands, calling for silence.

"Bring the prisoners!" Commanded the King. As the guards sped off to retrieve Marvel and Psychic, he took the opportunity to speak with the people. "We are all gathered here today to commemorate the many victories of my son, Jack the Panther, the Prince and the daughter of my most friend and brother, Pat the Python. The intruders will fight to the death and, if they win, they will get to take possession of the swords of their opponents. The rules..." the crowd held it's collective breath, "...there are no rules!" And the whole assembly erupted in a wave of ecstasy.

The guards who had gone to retrieve Marvel and Psychic had returned, and were marching the duo into the arena to prepare. Python and Panther were already waiting at the other end of the ring, clad in shining armor and, at their sides, the fabled weapons which the King himself had entrusted to them. The previous night's arguments had left them bitter, but full of renewed resolve to destroy their opponents. They were perhaps more dangerous than ever; fueled with rage and revelation about their past. "*I* may not be the true heir," thought Panther. " but I am the protector of this realm. I am incapable of losing to these mortals." This realization filled him with pride and purpose.

Python could see the fire in her best friend's bearing and tone. Nothing escaped her perceptiveness. After all, they had been friends since childhood, and she knew him better than anyone. She, too, was alight with the resolve of her revealed destiny. "No one can defeat us.' She thought, looking from Panther to their foes across the arena.

As Marvel and Psychic were placed in their corner, they exchanged a few words to ready themselves for the battle.

"Well," said Marvel, "another fight, another opportunity to stretch our legs."

"Listen, we have to take this seriously. We're a long way from home on a mission for the Almighty. We can't fail, and being to relaxed might get us killed."

"I know, I know. Look, we've beat these two before haven't we?"

"That was different; we're in their territory now." Chastised Psychic.

"Let's just get this done." Marvel shook his head as he tightened his gauntlet.

The crowd fell silent once more as the King lifted his right hand. The moment hung in the air like an executioner's sword.

Chapter 9

"Begin!" His hand came down with ferocity, and the fight was on.

Both pairs of combatants rushed for the middle of the arena, clashing with a thunderclap as their drawn swords sparkled in the sun.

Marvel had gone for Panther, and as their swords met in a flash of sparks and heat, Marvel smiled and looked into Panther's eyes. "You know, you don't seem to remember us but..." Panther shoved him away and rebounded off the wall of the enclosure, aiming a deadly swing of his sword at Marvel's head. Unphased, he parried the attack and locked his arm in Panther's. "You don't remember us, but we already defeated you on earth." Panther struggled slightly against Marvel's arm lock. He pulled Panther closer. "And we will do it again." He grinned.

Panther broke free, throwing Marvel into the air and catching him by the leg.

"We know who you are, mortal. What we don't know is what you're here for." He threw him aside casually, and as he recovered with a flourish of his sword, he raised his head to stare at his gloating foe.

"You may be surprised to learn that here our powers are two hundred percent greater than they were on Earth." Marvel showed no change in his countenance, staring with steely eyes into the face of his opponent.

"When we were in your weak and filthy human forms, we were severely limited. But now, we are endowed with all our might and splendor." Panther concluded with a wicked grin. He clenched his fist in an outstretched arm and it glowed with radiant heat and energy. Python, who had been fighting Psychic, saw Panther's display and smiled with renewed confidence.

"Shut up and fight me, damn you!" Marvel was having problems keeping up with the strength of Jack the Panther, though he tried not to reveal this. Panther's techniques where one of a kind and his speed was unimaginable. Disappearing in a blur, Panther slashed Marvel's leg with a sweeping blow right at the joint where his armor was thin.

"*Marvel!* Get serious, will ya!" Yelled Psychic, seeing the blow and watching as Marvel fell on one knee. "This is no time to play games! Let's finish them and go home!"

As she finished her sentence, Python rammed her fist savagely into Psychic's stomach, taking her breath away. Psychic retched violently and spilled blood on the ground. "What a punch." She thought as she stared at the crimson puddle before her through a blur of tears. Before she could even finfish thinking, she was hurled into the air and blasted with a fire ball that engulfed her in fire and agony.

The crowd exploded. "The battle is ours!" They shouted in unison. The king, Needrab, and the two mothers were ecstatic. They had overreacted; their kids could easily win this fight, they thought.

As Psychic tumbled through the air, smoking and burnt, her eyes met Marvel's as if in slow motion. "*It's about time.*" Their thoughts echoing in each other's minds. "*I guess so.*"

A low hum began to emanate from the two warriors. Between them was a resonance like the vibration of a tuning fork. Everyone who was watching fell silent as they struggled to understand what was occurring. The vibration was felt in the chests and in the ears of the whole assembly, and just as it reached a deafening roar, the whole arena was filled with a blinding light, and where the Marvel and Psychic had been, wounded and worn out, there stood two luminous beings of terrifying stature.

As the light subsided in intensity, Marvel appeared clad in bright orange armor that seemed to ripple and undulate across his body like liquid fire. Psychic had attained a flush, rosy armor that radiated with her true nature.

They spoke as one, with a vibratory intensity that shook Panther and Python to their core.

"We wanted to avoid using our true power." They boomed. "But it seems that we must reveal ourselves for what we are. *Holy agents* of the one true God."

The display of power from these two new warriors was overwhelming. So overwhelming that the crowd was on the verge of fleeing the stands entirely. The only thing keeping their fear in check was Panther and Python, who hadn't moved an inch.

"It is time to end this fight." Marvel and Psychic bellowed.

They seemed to explode from the ground, taking their opponents by complete surprise. Both Marvel and Psychic landed a blow on Panther and Python respectively that was so monumentally fierce, it split the stone underneath them. For a moment, the Prince and Pat were helpless. Python's arm was deeply wounded from the flying axe kick delivered from above, and it was pouring blood and burning in pain. Before she could recover, Marvel reaped her leg and slashed deeply through her armor into the flesh.

Somersaulting away to by time, Pat the Python and Jack the Panther switched tactics and changed fighting styles immediately. But the style looked familiar to the King.

"What are they doing?" Python began using the King's own signature style; she wanted to show him that *she* was his daughter. Jack began using

Needrab's fighting style. He, too, wanted his father to know that he was proud to be his son.

The fighting styles were so obviously copied from them that both King Suicufnoc and Needrab were confused, and wondered if there was a message behind these attacks. Then, they combined both fighting styles, displaying a wholly new technique, one which they had been working on for years. In it was a portrait of the inner feelings of the individual fighter, displaying a message to the King and the General.

There was beauty in the kicks, artistry in every movement, and they loved it. The message they wanted to transmit was received clearly. Needrab understood that Panther and Python knew about the secret, and King Suicufnoc felt an overwhelming feeling coming from Pat the Python. It was the feeling of a daughter crying out to her father. That is what he understood.

"We may lose this battle if we don't transform again." Communicated Psychic to Marvel telepathically. Marvel and Psychic had been overtaken by their enemy's new technique. Lying on the ground, bleeding and hurt, the duo only had one option.

Marvel shouted, "Fusion!"

The weapons of both warriors flew together and combined into a new, more terrible tool of destruction. It looked like an axe with two devilishly sharp blades, merged with a flail, a silvery chain draped on the ground; and the whole piece radiated a pale blue light.

It was all or nothing. No more holding back. Marvel and Psychic, wielding their newest weapon, flew forward with incredible speed to wipe their enemies from the face of existence. The weapon seemed to cut the very fabric of reality, bending light around it, becoming almost invisible as it came down to finish Panther and Python.

In the last instant, the King and the General came down from the dais and crashed into the axe-flail with their swords, barely deflecting the blow into the stone ground. The force shattered the whole arena, and would certainly have killed their children. The King and Needrab dragged both the stunned Prince and his best friend away from the fight before anyone noted what had happened.

King Suicufnoc said to Marvel from outside the ring. "Take the swords and get out of my kingdom!" He threw Panther and Pat's swords at the feet of the intruders.

"Father..."

"Silence, boy!" The King shouted savagely. "That's what you come for, now get out of my sight!"

Marvel and Psychic had not noticed, however, that Ynnafit and Siriey had covertly switched the swords with replicas in the confusion.

Pat the Python was able to stand, and walked over to the King to hug him tightly. "Father, I love you."

Jack the Panther limped over to Needrab and hugged him tightly, saying,

"Father, thank you for everything."

....

The crowd was not aware of details, they only knew the Pat the Python and Jack the Panther were not able to defeat their enemies. They were wondering why the King and the General had intervened. They could have won; still, they are great warriors, they thought. "Hurray! Hurray! Hurray!" The crowd cheered.

"We owe them an explanation, my King and husband." Said Ynnafit. "Let us retreat and sit down, the six of us."

King Suicufnoc was confused but relieved at the same time for their children. After all, it had taken tremendous energy to conceive them.

After they had retired to their chambers, they all explained the story from the very beginning to the King.

"I somehow felt that Pat was my daughter. I could see myself in her spirit. There was something deep in my intuition, telling me to acknowledge her, even though I did not know about your plot. Jack," he said tenderly, "you are my son and I love you. None of this changes that." Turning to Pat, he said in a loving tone, "My lovely daughter, you are just like your mother, cunning and fearless. I am so very proud of you."

. . . .

The two warriors, Marvel and Psychic, returned to their homes in *Moon Ville*, or, as many know it, Noom Live; holding the holy swords from the spiritual world of Nede Land.

They were not yet fully aware of what had transpired, or how these swords were in their hands now, or what they were supposed to do with them.

Chapter 10

*"For to one is given by the **Spirit the word of wisdom.**
1 Corinthians 12: 8"*

"I cannot find the old book. I honestly did not pay any attention. I think I threw it away. It was just trash to me." Said Decipher.

"Does it mean we have to go through all this garbage?" Asked Polyglot in disappointment. "With all the rotten food we had from the shelters, that is not something I want to do."

"Why all this hassle over an old book?" Decipher complained, throwing a scrap into the bin. "We should just locate that Guardian and beat the crap out of him."

"Do you know where the Guardian or the Secret Entrance are? Do you have *any* clue on how to look for them or find them?" Asked Polyglot, skeptically.

"No, I do not."

"Then there's no other option, is there, genius?" Polyglot kicked a pile of trash into the wind, angrily.

"Don't get mad, please. I was just thinking aloud." Pleaded Decipher.

"Let's get moving, the sooner we locate that old book, the sooner we can find the Guardian and get some exercise." He looked at Decipher and grinned.

"Strangely, I'm excited. It has been sometime since I used these muscles. I miss the adrenaline and battles."

"Remember, *patience*, my friend." Admonished Polyglot. "Patience and control above all. We left our old nature behind. Let us not succumb to it once again." As they began walking, he reminisced, "You need to keep your cool, man; you know you used to freak me out."

Suddenly, Decipher stopped dead in his tracks. "No way…no no no! That's not possible! Are you serious? I am about to run away and leave this task to you." Shouted Decipher.

"What? Why?" Asked Polyglot.

"Well it's just so important I thought you should handle it on your own." Quipped Decipher.

"Wait, are you being sarcastic?" Asked *Polyglot.*

"Look…" Decipher pointed to a spot in the distance.

When Polyglot looked ahead, he saw his answer.

"For crying out loud! Don't tell me the garbage truck already took the garbage!"

Decipher just giggled, shrugged his shoulders and said,

"I've never been to a dump, and now I have to go for an old dusty book. Please help me Lord! I mean, do you know how much garbage this small city produces? New Ville produces too much garbage on a daily basis, especially after all these restorations."

"Hang on, Decipher; you meant "*Newt Live*" didn't you?"

Decipher giggled. "Sorry man, I always forget that the city has a new name. My bad. Let's go to the dump then. Do you know where it is?"

"We will find out soon enough." said *Polyglot.*

. . . .

"Finally, after more than an HOUR, we found it." Said Decipher in an annoyed but relieved tone. "How are we going to do this? There is so much garbage and we have no idea where to start."

An old woman approached them and said,

"I have not seen you around here before, you must be looking for something important. You look very decent, not the types from around here."

"Old woman, is there any way to know where the last truck made its dump? We're looking for an old book that we accidentally threw in the trash. Probably all torn up by now I imagine."

"Why are you looking for this, *old book*, and what do you want with it? Why is it so important to you, eh?" Asked the old woman.

"It is an old book that tells of an ancient kingdom. It is a book of tales." said Polyglot.

"Well, hehe, I am a book lover of sorts and I always keep every book I find. I could show you the ones I found yesterday and today for a small price." Said the old woman with an upward glance and a grin.

"We have nothing to lose by checking them, and if you have it, we will definitely pay whatever price you name." Said *Decipher*.

"Do we have a deal, then?" Said the old woman.

"Yes." Both of them answered simultaneously.

"Something does not feel right with this woman." Thought *Decipher* to himself.

"Right this way. Follow me, please!" The old squeaked. She took them far from the dump.

"How far is your house?" Asked *Decipher*.

"Oh, you made a deal with me," laughed the old woman, "there is no backing down now; just follow me."

Polyglot and Decipher looked at each other, a little surprised. "What is this old woman talking about? I am starting not to like her." Whispered Polyglot.

"Yeah…" Decipher whispered back.

Suddenly, the old woman, who'd been walking with a cane up until now, stood up straight as a board. She hissed, "Boys, this is as far as you go." She removed her old rags as she spoke.

Standing in front of them, there was now a very beautiful, strong young woman, like none they had ever seen before. They felt attracted to her and willing to do whatever she wanted. She spoke in a lyrical voice, "Men cannot resist my charms. All men before you have bowed to my will. And now, so shall you. You boys have come to the wrong place and in your search for the forbidden kingdom."

At her last word, she blew a mighty wind from her mighty sword, and both Decipher and Polyglot were swept away from the spot and carried away down the road.

"I wanted to fight! But fighting a woman is not really my first choice." Fumed Decipher.

"Who is this gorgeous and powerful woman that wants to fight with us anyhow?" Puzzled Polyglot.

"I thought you were *Decipher*," the melodic voice of the woman emanated from behind them, "and you still have not deciphered this… I am disappointed. I was expecting more of an opponent."

Decipher, shaken, but in control, answered the criticism. "You have the wrong idea, woman. I knew since the very first moment you spoke to us that you were hiding something. After the first 10 words, I knew who you were. I was just keeping quiet to see what you were going to come up with…" He paused, "Guardian."

"Hold on, man. You knew she was the Guardian and you didn't tell me?" Complained Polyglot.

"My bad, man. I just wanted to see if she was going to ambush us.

"Wait a minute! You knew this was an ambush and you didn't tell me? Man, I am about to kick *your* ass instead of hers." Shouted Polyglot.

"Look, I'm sorry, but don't get mad. I was just playing her game." Soothed Decipher. "I don't normally fight women, but this one is an exception. Just sit down and enjoy the show." He winked.

Polyglot, after quelling his temper, responded, "Ok but, can I try her a little bit first, you know? It has been long time since our last fight and I might need some exercise too."

"How can I refuse an offer like that?" Decipher laughed.

"Hold on," said the woman, "you made a deal with me. I hope you are not planning to back down. Breaking a promise with me is not a good idea." She eagerly insisted.

"You got it all wrong, lady; We're not backing down. Besides the deal was that you'd show us the book and we still have not seen it."

With that, the dusty book fell from the thin air above them and landed gently in Decipher's hands.

"Oh, man! I think we messed this one up." said Polyglot.

"Don't tell me, there is not going to be a fight. Man, what a disappointment." Moped Decipher.

"You are two bloody rascals. Just looking for a fight!" Roared the woman.

"What is your price?" Asked Polyglot, remembering the deal. And the woman laughed, saying,

"Hilarious! Wonderful!"

"My price is simple, no need to worry about it. All you have to do is defeat my apprentices."

"What apprentices are you talking about? There is no one here, but you." Noted Decipher.

When out of the corner of his eye Decipher glimpsed a huge force-attack and he shoved Polyglot out of the way.

"Oof! That was a close one!" said *Decipher.*

When Polyglot looked up, there were two powerful men standing over him in fight position.

"That's what I am talking about!" Shouted Polyglot gleefully. "This is even better than gold. You have made my day."

"Defeat them and you get to keep the book. Lose and you will die." Warned the woman, casually.

"Well, I feel invigorated now." Said Decipher, sarcastically.

The woman sat down gracefully to enjoy the fight. She said to the duo, "Do not die on me just yet. At least give me a show for my trouble."

Chapter 11

When the woman finished talking, Decipher just sat down. He winked at Polyglot and they both laughed.

"Thank you for your kind gesture," said Polyglot with a grateful wave of his hand, "I am going to enjoy this one! You have just made my day, buddy."

"You are out of your mind if you think that you can take both of my apprentices alone." Laughed the woman.

"I will make you a new deal. Boomed Decipher. "It looks like you are very strong and I am in need of some exercise. Will *you* fight me if my partner defeats both of your apprentices?"

"You cocky man, you are way over your head. You think your partner will win this one? Two on one?"

"Are you accepting my new deal, or are you are too afraid to say yes?" Decipher said, slyly.

"Man, stop pushing it, she is scary." Polyglot pleaded.

The woman became enraged.

"I accept your challenge. Boys," speaking now to her apprentices, "kill that thug immediately."

Both of them dashed like lightning for Polyglot. There was no mistake, they wanted to end the fight right away. They were hitting so hard that he could not respond to the attacks. They quickly wounded him. As he bled, the woman hissed, "Kill him now." Both fighters said as one, "Time to die, my young friend."

They grabbed Polyglot and threw him to the ground like a ragdoll.

"Game over." Laughed the woman. Both fighters thought that Polyglot was dead. Decipher, however, was still sitting on the ground, quietly. He casually yelled, "Hey *Polyglot*, are you done playing with these two fools?"

Polyglot jumped to his feet and smiled, appearing not to have even a scratch on him.

"How is this possible?" Thought the woman angrily to herself. "And the two mysterious fighters…"

"Now?" Asked Polyglot. "Yes, buddy, you can stop playing now and fight." Answered Decipher, adding playfully, "Now watch this, lady. The real fight is about to start. I hope you enjoy it."

He was not done speaking when Polyglot hit both fighters with thunder-crack punches, and threw them on the ground.

"Where is all the strength coming from? He is so skinny." Thought the two fighters.

"Are you still wondering what hit you? Don't worry I wouldn't think too hard about it. Allow me to show you." Smiled Polyglot.

With that he leapt in the air and crashed down on them with a mighty blow, leaving them half dead.

"Done so soon? Man, I was expecting stronger opponents. I am so disappointed."

The woman was in a frenzied rage, yelling and screaming at her apprentices. "Weaklings! Get up and finish him now! He is no match for you two! I cannot believe you are embarrassing me with this skinny guy."

The two fighters got up, wearily and, summoning the last of their strength, attacked Polyglot for the last time. Their attacks glanced away from him without effect, completely impotent.

"Can you finish this already? I want to fight a little too." Yawned Decipher.

"Ok, how about a finished move?" Answered Polyglot.

"He is bluffing! How can he defeat my fighters with one blow? There is no power on this planet like that." Polyglot calmly turned his face to look at the lady and said…

"Watch me."

A fireball spread from his sword and spread throughout the glade, blowing the apprentices completely over. The two warriors lay on the ground; dead or unconscious, who knew.

"They were defeated by this skinny punk." The woman whimpered. "You are going to pay for this!" She leapt up and lunged at Polyglot with vengeance in her heart.

But, she met Decipher's sword gently resting on her cheek.

"No so fast, woman. The deal is that you have to face *me*. Are you backing down on our deal? Are you breaking the deal with us, woman?"

. . . .

Nobody knew much about Polyglot's background; he was an Israeli American man, young, about 26 years old. He was supposed to be the weakest one among his companions, but he'd proven to be an agile and fearless fighter.

"I have learned many disciplines in the past, having fought in every conceivable scenario. I am not proud of it, because I went through a lot of trouble, and suffered much. I had suffered far too many defeats, until one day, I told myself that I was not going to endure the bitter taste of defeat ever again. That is when I met the Lord. I now fight not with my own strength, but with the power coming from my faith in the Lord. I am blessed that He called me to be his warrior and I will not disappoint Him." Elaborated Polyglot, as he casually walked around the glade in which they had been fighting.

"I am not proud of my past either," said Decipher reflectively, "but the past made me who I am today. You see," now talking directly to the woman, "I was once called *Big Jax – the dragon*. I was trained by many masters, and was endowed with immense brute strength; such that *none* could stand against me. But I left all that in the past for the sake of my Lord. I have even forgotten the thrill of fighting, until now. Fighting here brings back memories…I feel quite nostalgic. Pardon me, Polyglot, but I want to feel a bit of adrenaline in my veins today."

Narrowing his eyes and leveling his gaze at the woman, "Do not disappoint me, lady."

"Enough with your chit-chat!" shouted the woman, "I couldn't care less about your sad stories or your past. The fact is, you're just stalling because you know you're no match for me. Prepare to die!"

In a flash the woman unleashed a flurry of attacks upon Decipher. The atmosphere itself changed and began to darken with her killer instinct as she moved. The air became heavy and smelled like hot metal. She was fearless.

"I am the Guardian of *Newt Live Kingdom* and you two will never defeat me or enter this kingdom!" She was crazed with violence and almost deformed from the anger.

"I'm not your opponent, so no need to include me in your statement." Chuckled Polyglot, mocking her.

"It infuriates me to hear you making fun of me! You are trying to belittle me, but you've made a huge mistake."

"More action and less talk!" Called Decipher, trying to make her even angrier. "Stop teasing her!" Warned Polyglot. "You're being too careless, taking hits like that. Just stop fooling around, we have things to do and I want to go home." He yawned.

"You always get like this when you are in a fight; you think it is a game! Stop having fun." All the while the fight continued to boil, with blow after blow charging the air with the smell of rage and glory. "We came from a dump for this fight, and the smell of the trash made me hungry."

"Have it your way," Decipher shouted, relenting to his comrade, "I'll finish this so we can go."

The woman rubified in anger and exploded with all her strength, making one last effort to kill Decipher. Shouting with each one of her powerful blows, spitting the syllables like bullets.

"*I - don't - care - if - you - are - or – were - a – dragon -, or – what - ever – trai- ning – you've - had, it – won't -change - the – out- come - of - this – ba – ttle!*"

Resetting her stance for a split second, she flashed an evil look at Decipher, saying, "You are going down and there is no question about it. Do you think I'm a Guardian for decoration? *I'm* the Guardian because scumbags like you never defeat me."

At that moment, as if answering her insult with pure strength, Decipher cleaved the air with his sword and blew her away with only the wind it produced.

"You're annoying me, woman. There's no need for bad language. I am not excited anymore. I thought you were stronger than me. I was expecting a big fight and all get is girl talk. Out of respect for you, I'll make this quick." He raised his sword one final time, and as it came down, it lit the earth aflame and swept the Guardian from existence.

Chapter 12

"We got so excited with the fight that we forgot to ask for the location of the Secret Entrance." Remarked Decipher, floating down to the ground.

"*You* got a little carried away," said Polyglot, a little annoyed, "You were supposed to ask all types of questions and get the Guardian to reveal the location of the Secret Entrance. Instead you crushed her completely. You always get carried away when fighting, even when training. You are so competitive and now we are clueless. I don't even know what happened to that old, dusty book."

"Are you referring to *this* dusty old book?" Giggled Decipher, producing the book from the folds of his coat.

"Excellent!" Exclaimed Polyglot, relieved. "We have to examine this book carefully to locate the message and the Secret Entrance."

"Polyglot," Decipher, confused, turned to Polyglot after thumbing through the book, "can you please have a look at this book? I do not understand a single word in it. I can only see images from the battles; strong people and great fights. I can see the woman from the dump here, and the two fighters as well….but there's someone else." He pointed to dark figure. "This dude looks strong. He is the one fighting in all the battles, and winning them too."

"Ok, let me read the book." Said Polyglot, taking the book from Decipher.

"I don't even know what language is this. It looks ancient." As he was squinting at the pages, all the letters began to rearrange themselves, and became understandable to Polyglot. He had received many gifts from the Lord, Tongues and Knowledge were among them.

"The book tells of a kingdom…a kingdom named… nae, nuw, tewn. Oh, I got it. It is called "*Newt Live Kingdom*"."

"That's weird." Mused Decipher, skeptically. "Are you making that up? That's the name of our city."

"I am not making this up; the name is the same, but it is a kingdom hidden from human eyes."

"Well, does it say anything about the Secret Entrance?" Asked Decipher, impatiently.

"Yes, it does, but you won't like it. It's located near where we first met the old woman."

"Are you telling me that we need to go back to that dump? A Secret Entrance…in a dump. What kind of joke is that?" Decipher was definitely not happy.

"No joke at all."

"Well, let's go, then." Said Decipher with a sigh.

"Are you sure you want to go now?" Asked Polyglot.

"Of course! I'm still excited from the fight!"

"Oh man, you never change." And with that, they set off in the direction of the dump.

When they arrived, the strong man from the book suddenly was waiting for them.

"Welcome, Decipher and Polyglot. I commend you on defeating the Guardian and her apprentices. I am impressed with your power. I hope to see it in action soon."

"Who are you?" The duo said in unison.

"No need for you to know for now. You have been granted safe passage to *Newt Live Kingdom*. You will see the sign and hear the door when it opens. But, before you go, I offer you a piece of advice: Your next opponents will be twice as strong as the Guardian and her fighters. Make sure you keep up with them, or at least give them a decent fight before dying." And the man ominously disappeared.

Decipher and Polyglot were now more excited than before. Stronger opponents mean more battles

"Awesome…" They both said at the same time.

New Ville

"I have a weird feeling. I don't know why, but for the past two days I have been hearing a strange ringing in my ears." Decipher sat on the edge of the porch in the fading light of day, the dusky sky framing his face with the grey-blue of puffy clouds on the horizon. He was fiddling with a piece of grass, twisting and crushing it between his fingers, releasing the volatiles into the air and filling it with that fresh-cut smell. "I cannot quiet understand it yet. I think it would be better if I could get Polyglot to join me for a BPF time."

He went inside to call Polyglot. He sat down and picked up the receiver to dial the number. After a few rings, Polyglot answered.

"Hey, are up for a BPF time tomorrow morning?"

"Always. 6 am at the church, as usual. Anything on your mind." Replied Polyglot.

"I'll talk to you about it then." Decipher said.

"You can count on me." And he hung up.

Decipher slept fitfully, tossing and turning in the night. When the dawn came he had barely slept. He decided to just get up and make his way to the church, since he couldn't rest anyway.

Polyglot was waiting in the narthex, absorbing the atmosphere of the house of God. "It looks like I am a little bit early." He looked down at his watch. "5:55. He won't mind if I get started."

"Hey man! Wait up!" Just then, Decipher came trotting up the stone floor to join Polyglot.

"Hey, I was just about to start; good timing."

"No kidding." Decipher commented as Polyglot continued to thumb through the Bible, waiting for inspiration to tell him where to begin. "So what's been going on? This may take a few minutes."

Catching his breath, Decipher took his jacket off and sat down. "Well, I have been hearing a ringing in my ears, but I cannot figure out where it's coming from. I feel crazy."

"Dude!" Polyglot stopped and looked at Decipher excitedly. "No joke, the same thing happened to me last night."

Decipher's eyes lit up with revelation. "It looks like it is time. The ring means that we are being summoned. Do you remember the lady at the dump?" Polyglot nodded seriously.

"It is time to start our mission. Let us pray." He added.

While they were in prayer, their eyes were opened to the new spiritual world and the door to the kingdom began to swing.

It was time for our heroes to start a new journey; a new adventure.

"Let us answer to the call and enter this new kingdom." Said Decipher with resolve.

With that, the portal opened fully, and a brilliant light pulled them in the vast realm which awaited them.

Chapter 13

Newt Live Kingdom

*"To another **the gifts of healing** by the same Spirit. 1 Corinthians 12: 9"*

The people of Newt Live Kingdom are proud of their beliefs and traditions. They call them "the eternal tradition", or "the eternal ways". They love nature and all that it embodies. The people are famous for learning from different types of animals, and they themselves believe they are descendants of amphibians, lizards, reptiles. They are experts in all aquatic sports and activities, having inherited or learned them from the water-dwelling creatures around them. They look after the reputation of the name of their kingdom, *Newt Live*, and are known as the head of *Anatanas*. *Kelddehi River* waters all the land, enriching the soil and making it fit for all types of agriculture.

Women in this kingdom are legendary. They are intelligent, beautiful, powerful, and cunning. Legend says that there was a time when a fearless woman took power, annihilating everyone that opposed her, and uniting all the people of the land.

Using her unsurpassed will and cunning tactics in battle, she completely wiped out all kinds of rebellions and uprisings, becoming the queen of the land. They say that her most trusted fighter, her *right hand*, is another fierce warrior who possess unbridled brutal force. She is called Inar.

Inar is always at the Queen's side, not leaving for an instant. When they are in battle, Inar is the ultimate weapon, and last resort along with Queen Aizar. They only engage in battle themselves when they see that their two most fearless warriors are taking too long to defeat their enemies, or if their rivals are so embarrassingly arrogant that they need to be taught a lesson, sending a very clear message to their future rivals. Patarp and Ijavish are the names of their warriors.

When they are not in battle, they are constantly training with the great Inar, which is supervised by Queen Aizar herself. They love to watch their warriors training and fighting challengers from the kingdom. That is how they demonstrate the invincible strength of their kingdom.

Inar loves to disguise herself as an old woman when enacting her plans. She likes to see firsthand how her victims look when she lures them into a trap.

One of her favorite schemes is to manipulate her foe into accepting an unbreakable contract or deal that completely undoes them in the end. Once she has them where she wants, she sits back and enjoys the show. She'll even call her two loyal warriors, Patarp and Ijavish to watch and enjoy as well. She loves to see her victims utterly destroyed.

On the other hand, Queen Aizar loves to disguise herself as a man. In the beginning of her fighting career, she pretended to be a man and fooled everyone. They all thought she was a handsome, powerful and young Prince. As the years passed and the Prince won battle after battle, his reputation grew. Until one day, while in the middle of a savage battle, the greatest of the enemy's fighters came close to beheading the young Prince. He was able to dodge the attack, but his true identity was revealed, shocking the people. It was the perfect opportunity for a wicked and conniving family to get rid of the young Prince for good.

In spite of all the battles won and the kingdoms conquered, after the people discovered her true identity, they demanded retribution. This animosity was instigated by an evil family that wanted to take over the throne, and so Aizar was banished from the kingdom. Inar followed her, as did two loyal warriors, Patarp and Ijavish.

After a time of wandering in banishment, Aizar found an old man to guide and train her in the ways of his kingdom. He taught her the Eternal Way, and all the secrets of the gods. Performing their tradition elevated her to goddess-like status, and she returned to the kingdom from which she had been banished as a Queen, but not before beheading the members of the cunning family and all possible heirs or rivals to the throne. The old man who trained her was a legendary warrior, never having lost a battle. His name was Natlus. He kept his true identity a secret from his new protégé, Queen Aizar, because he did not want anyone to recognize him and reveal his dark past.

They emerged into a field of tall grass, wafting in a gentle breeze. As their eyes adjusted to the bright light of the noon-day sun, they perceived two people sitting upon a knoll on the far side of the sea of undulating grass. Polyglot and Decipher approached the two men slowly, and carefully. They were perched atop a large flat rock, and appeared to be meditating.

"Namaste!" They shouted suddenly, and in perfect unison. Their eyes had shot open and they were now staring at our heroes. The duo jumped back, anticipating an attack.

"Welcome to the Kingdom of Newt Live. We have been expecting you." Said one of the men as he stood gracefully and made a gesture of reverence toward the pair. He was dressed in bright orange robes, the color of dawn, and a red sash around his waist. He looked relatively peaceful, sporting a wide but welcoming smile.

Polyglot and Decipher eased themselves and regained their composure.

"Thank you very much for your warm welcome." Said Polyglot with a bow. "It is our pleasure to be here." His tone was slightly sarcastic.

"Yes, we are delighted to be here. We came to your kingdom to fight your strongest warriors and take back what belongs to us." Decipher stated matter-of-factly.

"Can't you be more discreet? We should have tried to conceal our purpose from them." Polyglot remonstrated.

"Ah!" The other man burst. He stood swiftly and with energy. "We are very glad to hear that! Our leaders are quite aware of the prophecy, and we all know why you are here and what you came looking for. I am Patarp and this is my companion Ijavihs." They both bowed and made the same welcoming salute as they had earlier. "We will be escorting you to the palace where you will be properly attended and, when the time comes, our leaders will meet with you."

"See." Said Decipher. "They already know."

"I can sense a strong presence coming from these two men. But I cannot decipher the extent of their strength.' Whispered Decipher as the two men ran ahead a few yards and beckoned them to follow.

"Let's go with the flow and see what happens. They seem like very nice people." Added Polyglot.

On the way to the kingdom, they observed green fields with lots of livestock, and a crystal-clear river winding through the whole landscape. They had never seen anything like it before. It was the most perfect water, clean and teeming with fish of every earthly species.

"This is our largest river, and it is called *Kelddehi.* It is most rich in aquaculture, which is one of our specialties. Even though we are not one of the larger kingdoms we provide all kinds of seafood to the entire kingdom of *Nede Land.*" said Patarp.

They continued on their walk to the palace, enjoying the fields and the spectacular views.

"I can see this is a kingdom that is rich in agriculture as well." Mentioned Polyglot.

"Yes, it is. Farmed goods, livestock and seafood are the primary exports of our kingdom." Answered Ijavihs with pride.

"How far is the palace from here?" Asked Decipher.

"At this pace, it will take us approximately twenty-five more minutes. Normally, we have transportation for our guests, but our leader gave us explicit instructions to escort you on foot, so you can enjoy the view of the kingdom on your way to the palace." Patarp replied.

"It was gracious of your leader to organize such a lovely walk." Remarked Polyglot.

"What about these villages on either side of us?" Asked Polyglot

"These villages belong to the people working our fields and fishing in our waters. As they are closer to the fields and the banks of the river, they perform better." Answered Patarp.

As they walked around a bend in the river, they observed a few young women casting nets into the shallows. One of them happened to look up, the reflected sunlight glittering in the water illuminating her eyes, and caught Decipher's gaze. She gave a shy and subtle smile.

You uh, have some lovely women in your kingdom." He said absently as he craned his neck to follow her as they passed. Both escorts flashed a disdainful look at Decipher, and for the first time their glossy veneer of cordiality cracked. But in an instant, they recovered their demur and casual demeanor. Ijavihs wagged his finger dismissively and said "Yes, indeed, but it is forbidden to mix with foreigners; so don't get your hopes too high."

"You will not be here long enough to see anything else…" Patarp mumbled. Both of them giggled unsettlingly.

"Polyglot look to your right! You've got a see this." Decipher elbowed him in the arm, nodding his head emphatically to the right.

When Polyglot turned to look, what he saw was an incredible display of power. In a small cordoned-off area just on the other side of the river, there were a group of warriors fighting amongst each other. Observing them appeared to be a King and a Queen, perched on their respective thrones in the shade of an awning.

In the middle of the dirt arena, there was a single man who appeared to be fighting the rest of the challengers all at once. As they rushed him, he casually began to engage them, without the slightest indication of effort. With every swipe of his hand, with every strike from his powerful legs, the air itself buckled and sent a sonic boom through the area. Each of his blows would throw another helpless and overwhelmed opponent flying across the ring.

His muscles seemed to be made of granite, but his movements were as free as the water of the Kelddehi. Across his broad back was tattooed the face of a fierce lion, ready to pounce, and the name, *Natlus.*

When Patarp and Ijavihs noticed that Decipher and Polyglot had stopped to watch the fight, Patarp said "Do you want a better view of the fight?"

"Yes!" Both answered at the same time.

When they reached the arena to observe from a better advantage, they realized there was a large crowd gathered, but it had been obscured by the crest of the hill. They were all cheering and whistling for the beastly man standing amid dozens of defeated fighters with his hands raised in satisfaction. Enemies continued to pour in, and as he turned to face the side of the arena where Polyglot and Decipher were standing, they couldn't believe their eyes.

"Are you seeing what I'm seeing? Isn't he the old man we meet when we defeated the lady and her two warriors?"

"Yes, he is." Interrupted Patarp, "He is our Natlus; our hero. There is no one like him, and there are none who can defeat him."

Natlus looked around and saw our heroes. With a welcoming and ingratiating look on his face, he continued thrashing his opponents.

"This is an incredible man." Thought Decipher with excitement.

Chapter 14

After watching the display of power, which looked like it was organized for the sole purpose of curing Natlus' boredom and inflating his ego, the guests were taken to the palace.

They were taken to their rooms and attended on like royalty. Servants came to take their clothes to be washed, giving them robes of silk to wear to the bath house, which was a palatial indoor spa with a veritable lake of steaming water, bordered by limestone and granite pillars. There were oils and soaps of exotic origin in crystal decanters, and bowls of fruit chilled by cooling vents beneath the tables on which they were spread. Such opulence was overwhelming to the duo, who had never seen such things before.

The water, which was undoubtedly sourced from the river, had a rejuvenating effect on their sore muscles, and the sweet smelling oils relaxed their spirits.

"Are we in King Solomon's Harem?" Murmured Polyglot as he reposed in the steamy waters.

"Don't let your guard down," Decipher chided, "we have a holy mission to accomplish. Besides, they didn't bring us here to pamper us because they like us. They're trying to soften us up; make us slow."

"Chill, man, I'm just soaking up the good vibes." Soothed Polyglot.

"Still…"

Just then, Patarp burst through the heavy oak doors behind them.

"Enjoying yourselves?" He said with a strange smile.

"See?" Whispered Decipher.

"Tomorrow morning, after breakfast, we will take you to the *mandir,* or temple. You will be able to see our people in their full splendor!

"When are we meeting with your leader?" Inquired Decipher rising from the water and hurriedly throwing on his silk robe.

"Tomorrow afternoon." Patarp said curtly.

"You can go anywhere in the kingdom you wish, you are free to come and go as you please and none will hinder with you. You are *royal* guests. All you need to do is wear this badge and ribbon wherever you go. Everyone will know that you are guests in the palace." Patarp turned on his heel and left as quickly as he came.

The people in this kingdom are characterized by their calmness and *tenderness*; wherever you go people treat you with *gentleness*. The people have great faith as well, believing fervently in their various deities.

. . . .

"Decipher," Polyglot stated musingly, "too much gentleness is confusing to me. If they know why we are here, why are they treating us so nice?"

"I don't know, man; but so far, I feel like a king in the land of nobodies." They both laughed.

"Let us keep our eyes open, we don't know anything yet. We don't even know if we are going to fight that Natlus guy." Continued Decipher with an expression of disappointment.

"Relax, man. I am sure we will meet challenges beyond our imagination in this city. I feel that we will need to force ourselves to our limits." Reassured Polyglot.

"Let us hope that will be the case because I am kind of anxious."

The two decided to indulge in the freedom of movement they had been given, deciding first to explore the grounds of the palace. As they made their way down the winding stairwells and carpeted hallways of the inner keep, they emerged outside after passing underneath a large iron gate, which had several guards stationed within and without.

Beyond the gate, they found the sprawling gardens and rivulets of the palace, meticulously maintained, it seemed, by a veritable army of attendants. It seemed to be an endless expanse of the most vivid and magnificent colors they had ever seen. Lush and ruddy roses, peonies of the most exquisite violet hues the eye could withstand, and exuberant sapphire blossoms in row upon row encircling a grove of perfectly manicured shrubs.

Amid all this floral excellence, one flower stood out; it was a smoky, titian colored flower that held the quality of a flickering flame when seen from afar, yet, when one approached nearer the swaying plant. The surface of the petals seemed to alter in appearance slightly, taking on the strangest iridescence ever seen in a living thing. It maintained it's lovely saffron tint, and the almost charred looking edges of the petals, but the heart of the blossom shimmered almost imperceptibly with all the colors of the rainbow.

"What a fascinating flower, Decipher!" Exclaimed Polyglot.

"Namaste!" A voice from behind the two entranced heroes startled them. "I am Aizar, the Queen of Newt Live Kingdom."

"Dude, the Queen." Whispered Decipher in shock.

"Namaskar!" Answered Polyglot with a bright smile.

"Join me in our worship ceremony at the temple, so we can speak more intimately." The Queen offered graciously.

"We don't bow down to any God but our own." Said Decipher firmly. Polyglot nodded in agreement. "We don't mean to be rude or offensive to your hospitality, your majesty."

The Queen responded by waiving her hand, saying "We believe in many gods and deities, you are free to believe and worship yours if it pleases you."

Another woman had been quietly standing next to Queen Aizar, covered with a veil. They could only see her eyes. Somehow, the eyes were familiar to them both, but they could not tell who she was, and she did not utter a word through the conversation they had with Queen Aizar.

"We have been waiting for a foreigner to come from a distant land, one not of this kingdom." The queen related to them as they walked toward the temple. "We have finally seen the day. According to the prophecy, there is a warrior who will come, but instead of one, we have two. Ours is a kingdom of peace and tranquility, but we have four warriors that you must fight in order to gain access to our Secret Chambers."

The Queen continued as they walked, smiling at her subjects as they bowed before her and the *royal* guests.

"There are many treasures in our Secret Chambers and each one of you must defeat two of the four warriors. If you accomplish this, you will be able to choose one holy relic each. However, if only one of you is victorious, and the other fails, then you will only receive one holy relic. These are the rules; accept them, and we will set a date for a great feast in your honor."

Polyglot and Decipher had been listening intently. "So, you're telling me that each one of us must defeat two of the four warriors, is that correct?" Decipher asked with a flicker of excitement in his voice.

"Absolutely correct." The Queen let slip a slight smile when she noticed Decipher's excitement.

The Queen continued. "I see that you are not at all frightened by the thought of battle. In fact, it is something you are eager for. I sense excitement in your voice. The prospect of a fight has changed you both." She stopped suddenly. "Don't get excited. You will fight my best, and they have never lost." She moved closer to Decipher. "And they never will."

"If that is the case, then you have nothing to worry about, your highness." Said Polyglot in a sarcastic tone of voice. "We agree to your terms, your majesty."

Decipher shared his thoughts telepathically. "I wanted to rub it in her face that we have already defeated 3 of her warriors."

"Easy man! Easy! We are strong but there are too many to fight. We don't stand a chance fighting them all." Polyglot replied. "It is a grace that we get to fight only four. Don't tease the Queen or make her angry, she could behead us in an instant."

"Continue enjoying the pleasures of my kingdom with freedom, you will be notified about the time and place." Queen Aizar and her bodyguard departed directly.

Chapter 15

The Queen has never asked about the real identity of her protector, the great Natlus. All she knew was that when she was lost and in exile, she found someone to help her, nurture her, and assist her in retaking her kingdom.

From that day on, Natlus has been the protector of the kingdom and of Queen Aizar herself. He has helped her get rid of all the poison in the kingdom, including any family trying to oppose her reign. He is her most trusted servant, and he is like a father and mentor to her. Natlus, the hero of Newt Live Kingdom.

When Aizar was in exile, rejected by her people because she disguised herself as a man, she was all alone. Natlus found her and rescued her. All that is known to the people; what the people don't know, however, is that Natlus saw something in her, something he has not shared with anyone.

According to legend, the former Queen was killed along with all her subjects just minutes before Aizar ascended to the throne. They say that the sword that took their lives belongs to none other than Natlus himself. The people praise him and worship him, for he was the instrument of their liberation from tyranny.

It is said also that they had a king; a gentle and tender king who cared for and loved his people. Everyone in the kingdom loved him like a father, they say. People used to come from every corner of the kingdom seeking guidance and counselling from the great and compassionate king. He was like a god to the people.

But his wife's family opposed him, and plotted against him. On the night of the revolt, they charged him with false accusations, presenting witnesses from every part of the kingdom who testified that he was mad. They condemned him to a life in exile. They could not kill the king, because that would create too much chaos and division in the land.

After the false verdict condemning the king to a life in exile, no one ever heard from him again. As the years passed by, he was forgotten by many. Some say that there was a survivor of the king's family, a boy. But no one knows what became of that boy.

. . . .

On one of their excursions into the kingdom, Decipher and Polyglot found themselves by the Bazaar when they saw a group of ruffians trying to thrash some young men. The fight was meaningless, but the young men were beaten badly and the ruffians refused to stop. Decipher decided to intervene and defend of the young men, showing his strength and trouncing the ruffians.

Tables were broken and some stores destroyed in the commotion. When the police arrived, everyone defended Decipher and Polyglot, bearing witness to their good deed. The authorities took the ruffians away, and word of this heroic deed reached the Queen. She was pleased that our heroes had acted so valiantly.

The Queen summoned to attend a gala, where there would be a feast in their honor. The Queen utilized the opportunity to announce the date and time of the competition as well.

"The day after tomorrow, at ten in the morning, we will hold our most famous competition!" The crowd cheered. "Our honored guests will partake in it. I will allow them to fight four of our warriors to demonstrate their strength! In the first round, they will fight Patarp and Ijavihs." Patarp and Ijavihs bowed as the crowd applauded them.

If our guests manage to defeat them, they will fight Inar and *Natlus*."

Everyone was amazed that the two foreigners would have the opportunity to fight the strongest fighters in the kingdom. The right hand of the Queen and the hero of the kingdom. The people started screaming, "*Natlus, Natlus, Natlus!*"

To Decipher and Polyglot, it was a surprise because they defeated Patarp and Ijavihs on earth. They still did not know who Inar was but they surely knew about Natlus.

Nonetheless, they felt invigorated, happy, and excited. They were going to have at least one strong opponent to fight.

....

"Queen Maha, your husband is a self-righteous man! He is not allowing us to conduct our business as usual. With all his regulations and police patrols, raids and shut downs, we cannot operate our liquor businesses, pawnshops or money lending businesses. You are my sister and you need to make him understand that he is creating problems for our family. As your brother, I am advising you, but things are going too far, and I fear that we will reach the point of no return very soon. He is a good man, the King. He is a good husband to you and father to your child. He even takes care of the children he's sired with his concubines." Devi, who was pacing and agitated, was the Queen's brother, and felt it necessary to update her on the current affairs.

....

"My Lord and King, I am not asking you to overlook the transgressions of my family, but at least don't attack them directly. They are my family after all, and they have been conducting business for centuries. It is a legacy from my father." Pleaded Queen Maha.

King Iput responded harshly. "I am not going to compromise my integrity and the integrity of my family for the sake of those who wrong my kingdom. Your brother has tried to bribe me several times, and the only reason I have not beheaded him is because he is your brother. But if they continue shaming my kingdom and tarnishing my reputation, I will take serious actions against them, and finish their illegal businesses once and for all." At this point, the Queen's brother, Devi, who was hidden somewhere in the room listening to the conversation, snuck out to warn his family.

Devi, upon reaching his home, gathered up his loved ones and explained the King's position, and how they were about to lose everything. They were consternated and angry. They felt they needed to get rid of King Iput. What better way than incriminating him? That tactic had always worked for them in the past.

Devi summoned Queen Maha once again to share with her his family's plan, promising that she would be the sole ruler once the King was gone. She agreed to play her part in this dastardly plan, and they began constructing the details that very evening.

They paid off the police first, then they hired false witnesses to testify against the King, instructing them to accuse him of money laundering and co-participation in illegal businesses and profiting from selling illegal alcohol and drugs. They even planted illegal currency in the King's palace to incriminate him. Queen Maha ended up being one of the master minds in the plot, so desperately did she want to be Queen.

When the news exploded onto the scene in a masterstroke of media deception, the King was sleeping in his bedroom along with his wife, Queen Maha. She had instructed a group of her most loyal men to wait in the palace to arrest the King before he could call his personal guards. When the King awoke, and realized he was trapped, and that his own wife was part of the coup d'état, he was devastated.

He knew that his wife did not like his relations with his concubines, and cared even less for the children he had with them, but he asked her to forgive them and protect them.

"Yes, my love. I will make sure nothing happens to them. I promise they will be well taken care of in your short absence. I am sure this is all a misunderstanding." She lied like a serpent.

They took the case public, but the king was jailed immediately, so overwhelming was the evidence against him. The scandal shook the kingdom and riots broke out overnight, the leaders of which blamed the king for all the evil things and illegal activities in the kingdom.

"He is a liar!" They said. "He has lied to us all!"

There was only one family who advocated for him, saying that it was all a lie. But nobody paid attention, because all the high officials were corrupt and part of the plot to jail the King and exile him. In less than 48 hours, the King was jailed, tried, and convicted, and all on fabricated evidence. There was but one family on the King's side. The verdict was a life sentence in exile in one of the worst prison's outside the kingdom.

"We must wipe out any descendant that may claim the throne." Devi advised.

"Get rid of all the concubines and their children, none must survive." Queen Maha ordered.

They were all butchered without mercy. No descendant who could legitimately claim the throne survived that horrific purge.

Chapter 16

The day of the ceremony had finally arrived and people from all parts of the kingdom have come to watch the fights. Of particular note was a small family of 7, composed of the father, an elderly man in his late 90's; his wife, a woman in her late 80's; and their three sons and two daughters. Everyone welcomed this family, even the Queen. They were legendary followers who loved the king. In fact, this was the same family who had advocated for the king and defended his innocence. They were the only family left from the time of King Iput.

After killing the evil former Queen, the people discovered the truth of King Iput's innocence, and the people that made this possible was the small family in attendance today. Their only regret after so many years, was that the only heir to the Kingship was dead, and Iput's bloodline was extinct.

The father and mother were not usually present for events such as these, but when they heard that foreigners had come to challenge the kingdom, they were eager to show support for their homeland.

. . . .

The Queen strode across the platform in the east corner of the arena, and, arriving finally at the podium amid the furious cheers of her people, addressed them with noble dignity.

"Good people of this fine land!" After a tumult of pride for their Queen, the crowd began to quiet. "It is time for the ceremony to begin. For the first match, representing our kingdom, we have our very own Patarp!" Patarp stepped forward, and in his customary style, bowed to the stands. "Versus!" She paused dramatically. "Polyglot!" The people were ecstatic that someone had come to challenge their finest fighters. This time, it was not a challenge for their liberation, it was a fair fight for the enjoyment of pure, wholesome competition.

"In the second match, we have Ijavihs representing us! He is challenged by the outlander, Decipher!" Our hero stepped out onto the stage and waved to the uproarious people.

"Remember the rules, and fight like sportsman!" Exclaimed the Queen with a flourish.

Polyglot and Patarp made their way to their respective sides of the arena. When they came together in the center to shake hands, Polyglot leaned in and said to Patarp,

"Don't you remember me? I have already defeated you on earth." Patarp was unmoved. "It won't be different this time, you will meet your end today."

"You must be confused." Patrap replied in an icy tone. "You think that because you defeated my brother, you are going to defeat *me*. He was weak and had no resolve; that is why he lost."

"Brother, eh?" Polyglot said. "So much the better. I get to defeat both of you, except this time I will dispatch you with even greater ease than your brother." He laughed.

This last barb was enough to send Patarp over the edge. As Polyglot was laughing, he landed a savage kick to the hero's ribs, cracking one and bruising another. "That got my attention." Polyglot thought, rebounding off the ground. But before he had even finished recovering, Patarp landed another kick squarely in Polyglot's face, breaking his nose. Blood fell from his face into the sand of the ring as he sunk to one knee.

"That…was unexpected." Polyglot looked up, wiping the blood from his nose and cracking it back into place. What he saw confused him.

"Wait a minute! Is your brother back from the dead? I see two of you! He exclaimed in confusion. He shook his head. No double vision. "Man, he hit me harder than I thought. This dude is strong."

Decipher, watching from the stage, was casually waiting for his turn with his arms crossed. "Stop messing around and finish the fight! I want to exercise a little bit too, ya know!" He cried.

He surprised everyone with his comments. The Queen thought he must be bluffing.

Polyglot looked up and over at Decipher, smiled and said as he rose to his feet. "Well, I guess it's time to get real, then." He cracked his knuckles. Meanwhile, Patarp had launched into a flying round kick from across the arena.

"Not so fast, my friend." Polyglot grabbed his opponent's leg with his right hand and smoothly guided him straight into a bone crunching jab from his left.

"I can't afford any more broken ribs." He said as he threw Patarp to the ground. "Let's get serious, I know you are stronger than this. Show me what you got."

Patarp slowly drew his sword. "Well, I didn't want it to get to this point, but now…" He twirled his scimitar with deft skill. Polyglot drew his Messer sword, which radiated a strange and brilliant light. The light emanating from his sword blinded Patarp for a split second, and Polyglot took the opportunity to go for the kill.

Patarp met him in the air, anticipating the strike, and parried expertly. As Patarp landed on the ground, he perceived a splash of blood on the ground.

"Ha! I got you." Said Patarp.

"Are you sure? Look down, man." Suggested Polyglot. When Patarp looked he saw that *he* was the one bleeding. There was a steady stream of crimson coming from his right arm, and additionally there was a small cut on the right side of his face. He replayed the movements in his mind, trying to understand how it had happened, but he had no idea. He became enraged at this humiliation. He clenched his fist and whirled his scimitar furiously at Polyglot in a barrage of lightning fast attacks. But blow after blow proved ineffective as our hero skillfully, and easily deflected the onslaught.

"I'll give you this, you are stronger than your brother, but you are no match for me. Give it up!" Polyglot shouted as he swung his blade into his opponents guard, casting him aside like a defeated dog.

Polyglot sat down casually. A few seconds went by, and the Queen stood.

"Are you acknowledging defeat?" Polyglot retorted "Are you sure you are asking the right person?"

The Queen looked over to a shaken and bloody Patrap.

"You are indeed...strong." And with that, he disappeared.

. . . .

"Finally, it's my turn now!" Shouted Decipher, jumping up from his seat to greet Polyglot. "I thought you'd never end that man. What took you so long?" Looking a little beat up, replied "Just trying to amuse the audience." They both laughed and embraced.

Decipher took up his equipment and descended into the arena where Ijavihs was waiting for him.

"I am not going to be as indulgent or playful as my partner." Said Decipher. "I think I will end the fight in three moves. Come at me with all you've got!"

Ijavihs became infuriated by the implication that he would lose so easily. He charged Decipher at an incredible speed, but his anger clouded his focus, which revealed that he was even more easily distracted than Polyglot's opponent. He swung wildly, attempting with fury to land the most uncoordinated and sloppy combinations of attacks Decipher had ever seen. Decipher ducked one of the more obvious attacks and thrust his sword into Ijavihs's left leg.

"There's one." He laughed.

"My partner already defeated you on earth and I watched your movements. There is nothing new you can show me, it does not matter if you are the same person, a twin or a brother, the outcome is inevitable!" Shouted Decipher with glee. "Ah! You see…" Seeing another opening, he threw his second blow, this time hitting Ijavihs on his right leg.

Things were not looking good. He was now hobbling around and jumbling attacks together even more predictably than before.

"This is so lame." Said Decipher in disappointment. "I cannot believe I am fighting a weakling like you." With a final thrust of his kodachi, Decipher aimed to end the fight. Ijavihs was happy to see the attack coming, and attempted to block, but he failed to see that Decipher had faked him, drawing a second blade that he slipped between his ribs, killing him instantly.

"That's three." Decipher mumbled in disappointment.

Chapter 17

"The real fight is about to begin now." Said Polyglot
and Decipher in unison, smiling and looking at each
other in excitement.

"I want to fight Natlus." Said Decipher.

"Be my guest." Relented Polyglot.

Until now, Decipher and Polyglot had not seen the
face of Inar. They only knew that she was strong,
and that they would fight her, but her appearance
was a complete mystery. Natlus had been the focus.

"Not so fast, warriors." Said the Queen. "I
congratulate you on your victory." Her tone was
slightly sarcastic. "The match will not go as you
expected. *I* will decide who will fight who in the
next match."

"C'mon!" Yelled Decipher in dismay.

"Inar will fight Decipher." At that moment, Inar
stepped from the Queen's side onto the main
platform, ready to fight Decipher. Her face was still
covered; only her eyes were visible.

"What a disappointment, man!" Said Decipher,
kicking rocks. "I wanted to fight Natlus, but I guess

I will take this one instead." He turned to Polyglot. "Are you sure you can handle him?"

Polyglot looked back over his shoulder and winked at Decipher. As if to say, *I'll be fine.*

Decipher Looked out across the arena, expecting to see Inar in the distance.

"All right you…" But Inar was already airborne, flying feet first at Decipher. She made full contact and sent him flying.

"You're stronger than I thought. I feel better now," He said. "I thought this wouldn't be any fun at all."

But Inar didn't appear to be interested in banter. She relentlessly hammered him until his guard broke, taking the opportunity to slam him onto the ground. Decipher hadn't been able to throw a single punch. He had been blocking all her movements, putting everything he had into defense. Jabs to the face, kicks to the body; everything. Finally, bleeding all over, he tried to counterattack. But the timing was off, and Inar made sure he regretted attempting to strike her.

Inar spoke for the first time after she sent Decipher to the ground with a reaping hip throw.

"On Earth, I was limited in power, but you are in my kingdom now." She kicked him directly in the face. "I can use the full measure of my power. Now *I* am victorious." Two more crippling blows to his head. Unmoving, Decipher appeared to be dead.

Everybody cheered and rejoiced. Inar, the Queen's own guard, has defeated her opponent with brute force alone. She was magnificent.

Beaming with pride, the Queen made an announcement. "Now, let us move on to the next fight. But Polyglot interrupted.

"I don't think that will be possible, your Highness." The Queen, smiling with anticipation, turned to him and said "That is great news! The second warrior is accepting defeat before even facing the mighty Natlus!"

The crowd went wild, chanting "Natlus! Natlus! Natlus!"

"Excuse me…may I have your attention please?" Said Polyglot amid the uproar. "I fear you are mistaken. The reason why I said it would not possible to start the second fight, is because the *first* fight isn't over."

"What? Did you not see the…" As the Queen turned to point at the lifeless body of Decipher, what she beheld stupefied her into silence.

Lying on the ground, seemingly lifeless, Decipher seemed to rise without moving a muscle until he was standing on his feet. Except, the warrior who now stood before the stunned crowd bore little resemblance to the bloodied and beaten man who had been lying there a few minutes before. Clad in an armor that defied imagination, Decipher looked like the holy agent of God that he was. His helmet, breastplate, shield and footwear were cast in a metal not of this world, gold within blue within radiant light. He strode a few paces to place himself in the center of the arena, and his sandals pooled flames in his footprints as he walked.

"Behold my true form." He spoke in a reverberating voice that filled the stadium.

"You should be grateful that I have allowed you to see who it is you are fighting."

With his last word came a terrible sound, like a tempest raging from the center of the ring. He flew directly at Inar, slammer her face into the dust and ripping her cover to shreds.

"That's what I thought." He boomed. "At first I was skeptical, but no longer. I knew you were the mysterious fighter. Get up and face me as you did before."

Inar stood, and as the dust settled, it became clear who Decipher was speaking of. It was the old woman with the cane in the dump, the guardian from Earth.

"*You,* I have already defeated. You are stronger than before; I'll give you that. But it will not be enough to defeat me." He looked down at his chest, and a glowing #3 appeared. He grinned.

"You see, among our warriors I am the third in power. There are only two who can say they are stronger than me, and believe me, you do not compare with any of them."

Inar was red with anger now, and tried to end the fight by leaping into the air and coming down on Decipher with a hail of devastating blows, but it was for nothing. Decipher superseded Inar in every conceivable way. Strength, speed, agility.

He jumped back, deflecting a punch, and disappeared. The great light shining from his armor made him invisible to her eyes.

"I promise you this, Inar. You won't be able to see me until it's too late." A seemingly disembodied voice shook her to the core. She swung blindly into the air, hitting nothing. Decipher was right, by the time he was close enough to end the fight, it was too late. The invisible warrior, or the Blue Knight, came from the light and crushed her under his heel.

"Now *that's* what I call strong." Said Polyglot.

Chapter 18

Queen Aizar was not amused. Three of her best fighters were defeated, and her only hope for redemption was Natlus, the hero of the people.

"Do not fail me. These contenders are stronger than I thought. I am counting on you." Said the Queen to Natlus. The people starting yelling as he stepped into the ring "Natlus, the hero! Natlus the man! Natlus the father! Natlus the protector!"

"Boy," announced Natlus in a commanding voice, "you must transform as the other did. Give me your true strength from the beginning, I don't want to bore the crowd with preliminaries. I had originally wanted to fight your partner, but I suppose thrashing you will have to do."

"I've seen your strength, this is a fight I will enjoy." Responded Polyglot, transforming right there into the brown knight in full armor with His ruddy golden helmet, brown diamond shield, brown bronze breastplate, brown silver belt and brown Spartan sandals flaming at the heels.

"You wanted it, and now you've got it." He said confidently. Polyglot knew that he needed to use his full strength against Natlus, or risk being undone, and Natlus knew it too.

Polyglot wasted no time, springing into the ring and activating the sparkling diamond shine of his messer sword to blind Natlus. But his opponent blocked the initial attack and struck Polyglot with a crippling elbow to the stomach.

Polyglot recovered almost imperceptibly fast, and redoubled his effort to bring down the mighty warrior.

"The Lord is with me." Thought Polyglot as he threw blow after blow. "He is my shepherd."

BAM!

"My high tower."

CRACK.

"My sword."

BOOM!

None of his blows landed any damage upon the seemingly invincible Natlus.

"Allow me to repay your gratitude." Natlus grabbed Polyglot by the neck suddenly, and drove him into the dirt, pushing him along like a human plow. He grabbed the messer still in Polyglot's hand. "I'm going to dig your grave with this silly weapon."

"I don't think so!" Polyglot wrenched his arm free and spun in the air to get away from his foe.

"The outcome is inevitable, boy!" Jibed Natlus. He disappeared in a cloud of dust and reappeared next to our hero, and before he could react, Natlus began an agonizing barrage that left Polyglot unconscious.

As Polyglot's fate seemed soon to be sealed, there came a voice from the stands. It was the old man, the advocate of King Iput.

"Long live King Iput! Long live the King!"

Initially, no one paid any attention to the senile exclamations of the old man.

And as Natlus was about to use his killing stroke on Polyglot, who was unconscious in his grip, he met Decipher's blade in the air.

"Not so fast." Decipher said. "I cannot allow my friend to die here. I will fight you."

Just as Natlus was about to turn and oblige Decipher, Queen Aizar stood up.

"The fight is over! Natlus is the winner! There will be no more fighting today, our guests have won the right to claim one holy relic. Go, attend your companion." Speaking to Decipher, who obeyed.

The old man approached Natlus after the competition and said "You are the true King; *you* are Iput Natlus, the only true king of Newt Live Kingdom." Trying to wave the man off, and dismiss him as insane, the old man ripped Natlus's shirt, revealing the mark of the king tattooed on his back. The mark of the exiled, and the mark of the prison were next it, proving the old man's story. A few people in the immediate vicinity started shouting that the King had returned. These few turned into a hundred, then a thousand, until the whole of the city had fallen to its knees, pledging fealty to the one true King.

"The King has returned!"

"We almost lost hope," the old man said, "but I knew you would return and avenge our kingdom. Now I rejoice because I know you have done so. You can cleanse the kingdom of all these rats that are poisoning it and return us to glory. It is a shame that your descendant did not survive."

"Stand up my friend, everything is forgiven. I have no desire to be King, we have a Queen and she is my descendant." The old man's eyes went wide. "Yes, she was the only survivor on that fateful night. That is when my allies starting thinking that she should dress like a boy, and so she pretended to be a boy to conceal her identity." Natlus said. "Show them the sign of the kingdom, my daughter." Speaking to the Queen.

The Queen stood and showed them the mark that only the direct descendant of the King could bear. The crowd gasped and rejoiced.

She said "Father, you never revealed yourself to me, but you were always by my side. Why did you not reveal yourself?" Tears were streaming down her cheeks.

The former King replied. "It was necessary for the kingdom and for your protection. I needed to get rid of all the poisonous people, and you have proven to be a most worthy successor, child. I am glad I have been able to train you and mentor you." They embraced and wept together as father and daughter with the whole kingdom rejoicing for them.

. . . .

The next morning, after a great feast of love and light, Polyglot woke up from the thrashing he received.

"I'm sorry, man. He was just too strong. I thought I could beat him." Polyglot clearly felt ashamed.

"Don't worry, friend." Soothed Decipher. "Let us claim the prize and get back home."

Queen Aizar and King Natlus were expecting them when they came to claim their prize.

"You have earned the right to enter our Secret Chamber and select your reward."

When they entered the Secret Chamber, there were many relics indeed, but none of them were the ones they were looking for. Decipher saw something glittering, twinkling below a mantle on the wall. When he uncovered it, there was a shining sword underneath with an inscription that read *The Gift of Faith*. Next to it there was another sword that possessed even greater power that called to them. The inscription upon the hilt read *Tenderness*.

They were going to select the second sword at first, but they were stopped.

"You have already chosen your prize and you cannot change your mind now." Said Natlus gently. Decipher was not ready to let it go, but Polyglot told him,

"There will be another time, let us go."

They understood how this kingdom was stealing from humanity, and hindering it from retrieving the *Gift of Faith*. Decipher said, "That is why humanity is losing its faith in the only and true God, because you were holding it from us. We will take it back home and restore the faith humanity has lost. We will help them reconcile with our Lord God. But make no mistake," he continued, "we will surely be back for the second sword."

"We will be expecting you." Said Natlus with a calm and tender voice.

Natlus and Queen Aizar understood that the prophecy spoke about someone else as well, and there was yet another fierce battle to come....

Chapter 19

Blue Ball

Shrewder was an incredibly wise man. He had
already located the ancient book they were all
talking about. The book disclosed details about the
hidden kingdom. He even knew the location of the
Secret Entrance and the identity of the Guardian.

He did not share this information with anyone, not
even with *Faith-Woman*, because of the possible
terrifying consequences of fighting the Guardian.
He saw the Guardian in the book and he knew how
fearless he was. No one noticed the true power of
the Guardian or "the peasant warrior" as everybody
in Babul-Ell called him. But from Shrewder's
perspective, because of his interpretation of the
book, the Peasant Warrior was the real deal, not
someone he wanted to face or deal with at all.

As a matter of fact, the Guardian himself gave the
book to Shrewder, and after reading it, Shrewder
knew exactly why.

When Faith-Woman came to Shrewder, asking him
to start searching for the book, he decided that it

was time to share all he knew about this new kingdom and the Guardian. He showed her the book and explained its meaning. In response, said to *Shrewder*,

"Well, let us find the Secret Entrance, it is time to face the Guardian."

Shrewder had his reservations, but he did not explain this to Faith-Woman.

"I know where the Secret Entrance is and I also know who the Guardian is." He said. When Faith-Woman heard these words, she rejoiced, because she knew they only needed to go to the Entrance and defeat the Guardian.

"Listen, I honestly don't want to fight the Guardian. This is a fight that I fear I cannot win." Lamented Shrewder.

"Don't say that. I have full faith and confidence that we will be victorious." Faith-Woman reassured.

. . . .

Hello Shrewder, I have been waiting for you a long time. I was beginning to think you would never show up." The Guardian smirked. "And who is this precious woman that came with you?"

"My name is Faith-Woman, and I am here to defeat you, Guardian!"

Shrewder did not utter a single word.

"Allow me to ask your personal perception of the current situation, Shrewder. Do you honestly think you can defeat me? How many of you would it take to defeat me?" And the Guardian threw a fist into the air, the shockwave from which shook the whole place.

When Faith-Woman saw this, she started to tremble. Shrewder decided to speak.

"There is no need to panic, Faith-Woman, just breathe, and trust in the Lord. Be true to your name and embrace your faith and the trembling will fade."

Shrewder and Faith-Woman were now ready to fight, and they had no intention of losing the battle, even though they feared they could not win. Their faith and hope was greater than any enemy they could face.

All of the sudden, the Guardian said,

"No one from this kingdom knows my name or even knows who I really am. Allow me to introduce myself properly; I am Larey, and I am the Guardian of Babul–Ell Kingdom. No one can gain access to the Secret Entrance but me. There are only two ways to gain access. The first way is to defeat me, and we all know that is not going to happen." He seemed amused with himself.

"I did not know your name; I only knew that the people in your kingdom call you "Peasant Warrior."

During this exchange, unknown to Shrewder, Faith-Woman was not able to move her body. Her limbs were not responding to her because of the sheer strength of the Guardian.

Then Shrewder said,

"I must ask you, what is the second way to have access to the Secret Entrance?"

"Only by my invitation, and I have never invited anyone to come to Babul-Ell Kingdom. I have never found a warrior worthy enough to receive this honor." The Guardian bowed. "I have good news for you two, though; I am not here to fight you. But if you want to fight me, you should know that, at this stage, the outcome would be your defeat. However, I have seen something growing within you and I can see your true potential. *I would like to train you to be worthy of entering Babul–Ell Kingdom."*

Almost relieved, Faith-Woman blurted, "Praise the Lord for this great news!"

"It is an honor for you to consider us, mighty Larey." Answered Shrewder, humbly.

"Go home, rest. We start at dawn. Once your true potential and skills are sharpened, I will tell you why I have made the decision to train you in the ways of Babul–Ell Kingdom."

....

They did not know what kind of training they were going to receive, but they were sure they wanted in. They wanted to be stronger. They wanted to be stronger than the Guardian Larey. Shrewder and Faith-Woman showed up a little earlier than agreed and the Guardian was surprised.

"I didn't think you'd come, I thought you chickened out, but it looks like this is going to happen. I am glad. I've wanted to do this for a very long time." Said the Guardian, smiling. "The training is going to be hard, unlike anything you've seen before. You must endure and see it through to the end. Originally, there were three stages to the training; unfortunately, you can only endure two stages on earth. I will guide you so that, when the time comes, you will be ready.

"You will need to pay close attention to my moves and emulate them. To learn from them and it is the goal for the first stage of the training. To complete the first stage, you will need to control three things, which you will discover while training. Be careful, I am going to withhold my strength, because I do not want to kill you. The more you grow, the more I will increase the level of my strength with you during training."

The training started immediately, and lasted for hours.

Shrewder and Faith–Woman were constantly exhausted. Several weeks passed by without discovering the three elements to complete the first stage of the training.

"You still do not understand," said the Guardian. "That you need to see the beauty in my movements and learn from them. You see, I *believe* in my skills, I have *control* over them, and I can *endure* any type of attack. The harder the better. Until you can manage these three elements of your training, you will not pass to the second and final stage here on earth. Time is short. Time is of the essence. Your time is running out." Pressured the Guardian.

"Fight, focus, concentrate, assess, analyze, attack, block, coordinate. Beat them savagely!"

After two more weeks, they were finally able to grasp the meaning behind their movements and improve their skills.

"We have finally passed the first stage. Let us start with stage two." Demanded Shrewder.

"Not so fast." Scorned the Guardian.

"You need a few days to continue your training and to practice the first stage. Meet me back here three days from now to start the second stage."

Chapter 20

Three days later the team was back on track and ready to continue the training. They'd had enough time to master their new skills and were eager to fight the Guardian, or at least *train* with him. They received their wish, and were speechless with the strength coming out of the Guardian, even though he was merely sparring with them.

"You already know the process, now we are increasing the difficulty. I will fight each of you, one at a time. While I am fighting one of you, the other will be observing and studying the grace behind my movements and skills. It is supremely important that you use all your strength. Stop concealing your real power! Don't you know that I am quite aware of your true potential? Stop restraining yourselves!"

The fights were fearsome, and for three more days they learned the second stage.

"You two are a little reckless. It is not only about fighting your opponents. You need to be aware of everything around you. Understand that your full strength must come from within. Do not rush into the battle. Observe, watch and learn from your opponent, then decide what kind of attack you will use. You need to master all of this in a matter of seconds. It only takes a second to lose your life in battle." The Guardian stepped back and placed his feet in a new stance.

"Watch me, I have total control over my opponents when fighting, but I show them *mercy.* There is *tenderness* in all my movements and attacks, but most of all, there is *humility.* The attacks do not come randomly, there is a technique and a purpose behind each one. With my movements, I am discovering my opponent's weaknesses and creating openings that may end the battle. Remember, it is all about results, not theory. I do not need to use all my strength, first I need to find out how strong my opponent is and then I can decide how to face him."

Two days later.

"Congratulations Shrewder and Faith-Woman, you have finally completed stage two. You are ready to enter Babul–Ell Kingdom! Remember, there is still much potential hidden within you, but you will need to discover it for yourself."

"And how about stage three?" Asked Shrewder.

"If you are brave enough, if you develop your skills continuously and discover the power within you, you will face stage three in Babul–Ell Kingdom

After the training, a few weeks passed by and the team was constantly preaching and evangelizing. Their faith was increasing and their commitment to the Lord was v deepening with each passing day.

Meanwhile, our two heroes, alongside the missioner's team, have been preaching feverishly, reaching souls and winning them for the Kingdom of our Lord. After receiving training that made them ready to start the new journey, they had only to wait for *the call.*

The team had mastered the main two stages of their training, and thus were able to use, at full potential, six primary pieces of the biggest puzzle. These were *Mercy, Tenderness, Humility, Belief, Control, and Endurance.* Yet, they were still not fully ready for what awaited them; There was still one more stage for them to master, but it cannot be taught on earth.

As they waited, they continued their training on their own, while also helping other leaders conquer whatever is left to conquer in the city. From demons and evil powers to intellectual and spiritual tests, nothing posed even the slightest challenge to these highly trained heroes.

'Shrewder, what do you think about dedicating some time in BPF?" Asked Faith Woman.

"You mean Bible, Praying and Fasting?" He replied.

"Exactly! You are learning." Said Faith Woman.

"Let us have it tomorrow at 6 am." Offered Shrewder.

"Sounds good to me, we'll meet tomorrow morning."

Babul Ell Kingdom

*"To another the **word of knowledge** by the same Spirit. 1 Corinthians 12: 8"*

The citizens for Babul–Ell kingdom have always been proud for their knowledge, their beauty, the strength of their men and, most of all, their name. They bow down and pray several times a day, using the positioning of the sun in the sky as their guide. Their faith is unmatched.

Posin is the name of the river that provides water to all of *Babul–Ell Kingdom*. The source of the river is high up in the mountains where it gathers life giving minerals which give strength and vitality to all the peoples of the land below. There is a richness of gold that is supplied by the river as well, and nobody but King *Babul–Ell* knows exactly how or why the river seems to be inexhaustible. In reality, the river holds a secret.

According to the legend, there was once a great warrior in the land that defeated all who challenged him. Many attempted to defeat him over many years, but these attempts were futile.

The warrior became tired of fighting opponents that did not possess the strength to defeat him, and so decided to create his own kingdom of peace and harmony, hoping that among all those who were drawn to his kingdom, there would be at least one who could give him the challenge he so desperately desired. As time passed, people of all the surrounding kingdoms came to live and dwell in his great land. Many pledged their allegiance to their new King, and in return they enjoyed a peaceful and prosperous life, for he was a good King.

Those of fighting age received training in the ways of the mighty warrior, not just to provide for the defense of the kingdom, but also because the King was looking for faithful comrades to serve in his Elite Guard. His name was *Babul–Ell,* and he named his kingdom after himself. The name means *"gate of God"*. The young warriors who were skilled enough and worthy enough to be guards of the house, carefully trained and selected, had to endure several tests and attain special skills for the kingdom.

The King met many women that migrated to his kingdom, but only one of them would become his beloved one. One day, she conceived and gave birth to a very handsome boy and the King named him *"Ell"*. The boy grew in wisdom and in strength, surpassing all the boys of his age in battle and intelligence. He was skilled and fearless. By the time he turned 12 the boy was already a gifted fighter, and his teacher could no longer compete with him.

The King, who had carefully observed the development of his son, rejoiced with pride on the day he learned that he had defeated his instructor. He decided that day to start training the boy himself, since there was no match for him in all the kingdom.

Chapter 21

Socially, Ell was a very likeable boy, possessing charisma and charm. He was also playful and had many friends that he would frequently go on adventures with. One of them, Larey, was a simple peasant boy who became friends with Ell in childhood, and they had remained friends through many years. He was Ell's best friend and partner. Whenever Ell needed to train, *Larey* was the one to train with, matching Ell's skills almost completely.

When the King called Ell to start training with him, they needed a skilled partner for Ell, and there was no better match than Larey. As the days passed by, and Ell's skills became more and more refined, it became apparent that he would soon match his father, Babul-Ell, at least in their sparring matches.

But Ell needed to prove his strength in real battle, so the King decided it was time for him to invade a neighbor kingdom. Ell himself only wanted to find worthy opponents against which to test his strength. He was not interested in wealth, status, or land; Ell was only interested in finding the best fight of his life.

Ell's reputation grew each day. He conquered four kingdoms in one season, defeating the finest warriors they had to offer. The whole of his father's great empire knew of the exploits of their prince, and were proud.

After a time, the wise King Babul–Ell decided to trust his son with the defense of his greatest treasure; something no one knew existed. Ell, the great Prince, was appointed as the Guardian of *the secret treasure chamber.* Babul-Ell told him that someday a worthy opponent would appear and try to steal the knowledge that was kept in the secret chamber. Ell would need to defeat this person no matter the cost, and since *Ell* was undefeated, the Prince doubted that anyone from any of the kingdoms would dare to challenge him, let alone defeat him.

When Babul–Ell told him the story, he was overjoyed, because he could sense, for the first time, a trembling tone coming from his mighty, undefeated father. Ell thought to himself,

"If the King is worried, it means the opponents may be worthy of defeating me."

....

Word came to the four kingdoms about *the secret treasure chamber* that Ell was guarding, and that whoever was able to defeat Ell would receive a huge reward from King Babul–Ell that he would bestow in person. Of course, no one dared to challenge Ell, but the prospect of a reward (gold, a place in the house, the hand of one of the King's daughters, earning a place in line to the throne.) was a temptation difficult to resist.

The four kingdoms each started preparing their best fighters, hoping that one day they could defeat Ell and inherit Babul–Ell's kingdom.

Since this was a great task for Ell, the King decided to send Larey to guard the Secret Entrance to the kingdom, the only passage from earth to Babul–Ell's kingdom. The confidence the King had in Larey's skills was equal to that which he placed in his son's. There was no one better than Larey for such an important task. The King knew that no one would defeat Larey or gain access to the kingdom.

That was the King's secret weapon, Larey and Ell. No one ever understood why such a powerful King, undefeated across all kingdoms would place fighters such as Larey and Ell in such positions. Some started to think that there was something else behind all of this, but no one, not even Larey (the peasant warrior) nor Ell (the King's son), knew for certain.

. . . .

Larey had a family, once, when he was very little. He could barely remember his parents; all he had were some vague, though happy memories about a man telling him something he could not remember, every day. He had suppressed the rest of these memories, though.

He was only 6 years old when Ell became his friend. After that, all he could remember was being in Ell's shadow. As an adult, he had some weird feelings concerning humans. He felt as if he were one of them, even though he knew he was not.

On one particular adventure with Ell, they made a tour of all the kingdoms, and they knew many girls in many taverns in each kingdom. They had many fights as well, and had much fun. But Larey would always sneak out to see the poorest part of the kingdoms they visited; places where no one would dare to go. He'd always had a thing for the "scum of society" as it were. And after many years of being the Guardian of Babul–Ell Kingdom on earth, his feelings of sympathy grew stronger. So, he decided to sneak into the human cities disguised as one of them.

On one of these earthly excursions, he encountered a very lovely and gorgeous woman. For months, Larey could not get her out of his mind, so he decided to pursue her. They formed a loving relationship very fast, and after some time the woman conceived a child. She named the child after his father, not knowing who he really ways.

The child's name was Larey , and he was from a small, forgotten town on earth.

News came to the ears of King Babul–Ell about Larey's adventure. He advised Larey not to share stories of the adventure with anyone. The King would take care of this himself. He did not want his warrior to be distracted. One night while the mother of the child was sleeping, King Babul–Ell paid her a visit, and that would be the last night of her life.

Next to the woman, the King saw this small child and thought "Little Larey." The King cursed the boy's skin, and left him to die in the empty house.

A few weeks later, King Babul–Ell received news that the child had indeed passed away and he forgot about the matter entirely.

Chapter 22

The father of the child learned about King Babul -
Ell's actions and conceived a plan to conceal the
child from the King. He had someone declare the
child dead to avoid further issues. Larey then took
the child with him and raised him, pretending to be
his uncle on earth. This was Larey's great secret.
Larey decided to change the name of the child as
well, and renamed him *L. Junior*. The child was
never told what the "L" in his name stood for. It was
forbidden for him to ask these types of questions.

The child lived his early years in sickness as a result
of King Babul–Ell's curse. No medicine or doctor
could cure the child's skin, which oozed with pus
and blood. For three months out of every year the
child was severely ill. His skin swollen; pus and
scars all over, and a constant itch that he would
scratch until he bled.

Three more months of the year, the child's skin
would create hard, thick scales like *corns* all over
his body. For three months after that, the scales
would become sticky and soft and more revolting

than before. It was only in the remaining three months of every year that he would heal and become somewhat normal.

Larey suffered also during these years, but he never gave up on L. Junior. As soon as L. Junior was able to hold a sword, Larey started training him and teaching him the ways of Babul–Ell Kingdom, despite his illness, but without telling the child the truth of his origin.

L. Junior did not have many friends or much time to make acquaintances due to his physical conditions. Skinny and sick almost all year around, kids in the neighborhood called him many names, but there was one that L. Junior kinda liked. "L.*J. Rash*." So he started to use this name around town. L.J. Rash was a nobody. He had no family, no background, he was just a poor boy with only an uncle who nobody knew very well. He was nothing. There was only one boy who used to visit the city and play with him as an equal. He showed love and compassion and never judged him. That boy's name was Ben.

Could something good ever come of L.J. Rash? They even called him "the corpse," because everybody thought he would die soon.

L. Junior developed a friendship with Ben and he was always excitedly expecting his visits. Ben would always go on about his God, and spoke constantly about His power.

When L. Junior turned 17 years old, Elohim called him to serve Him and follow Him. As a result of the calling, he was L.J. Rash no more. His skin was healed and when Larey heard the news he was overjoyed. "It was a miracle." *L. Junior* told his uncle, or at least that is what he understood. Larey did not know what had happened to his son, but he didn't care why or how he had been healed. He embraced his newly healed son with years steaming down his face. "My boy! My dear boy!" Larey picked him up and hoisted him high into the air.

"I feel...normal, uncle."

"As well you should, my...nephew." Larey composed himself and threw his arm around L. Junior. "This calls for a celebration." As they walked off to find a good tavern to enjoy a meal at, a dark cloud overtook Larey's heart.

"This changes nothing. I won't be deterred from my quest." He thought as they continued on, into the fading light of sunset.

One of the greatest kingdoms in all Nede Land, Babul Ell is only surpassed by the Capital of Nede Land itself, Hont Well.

Posin river, holding secrets and power as yet unknown to many, bestows many blessings upon the people of this kingdom, who consider it a great privilege indeed to be enriched by its waters.

It is said that Posin river holds the most precious and expensive mineral in existence. This was one of the main reasons the great King Babul Ell wished to conquer the land for himself.

In the early days, the mighty Babul Ell had a master and teacher, someone who taught him everything he knows. The Master was proud of his apprentice, and consequently sent him into the world to test his skills. There was no match for Babul Ell anywhere he travelled, and after he returned from his journey unsatisfied, weary of fighting such meaningless opponents, his Master gave him the idea to settle his own kingdom, with the promise that one day, Babul Ell would meet his destiny. A warrior worthy of his strength, willing to fight him.

That was a great promise, and it is what has kept Babul Ell going all these years. By the sixth year of his reign, Babul Ell received an invitation from his Master to accompany him in a crusade to besiege and wipe out a group of troublemakers from Nede Land. There was a condition though, the mighty Babul Ell would need to hide his true identity by wearing a set of armor that completely covered his features. No one was to know the name of the terrible warrior who did the bidding of the Master.

On the day of the siege, both the Master and Babul Ell wiped out an entire army from one of the kingdoms, leaving no remnant, not even a descendant who could carry on the legacy of those people. *Or so they thought.* On the battlefield, there was a renewal of vows from master to student and from student to master. This new covenant would seal the fate of humanity.

As part of the covenant, the Master gave Babul Ell his own son to train and raise as his own. That was the greatest honor, and most important part of the pact, and moreover, it was a secret that only they knew. That very same day, while the battle still raged, Babul Ell saw greatness in a boy from the village. After witnessing his whole family slaughtered, the boy tried to fight back and one of the guards nearly killed him. Babul Ell saw how fierce this little boy was and gave the command to spare him. He took pity on the child and from that day on the child was under his care as one of his own. After all, he needed someone for his new son to play with.

After completely wiping out the entire village, killing everyone in sight, they dubbed the act of brutality and, consequently, this ominous word became the name of the group whose identity was

"The Snaitsirch Group" completely wiped out from the Nede Land. Everybody went their own way, never knowing the identity of the unspeakable warrior, nor did they know that he had taken one child from the battlefield. Only the Master knew what had transpired.

A small group of defectors, who had come to the Master before the battle to give up their comrades and valuable tactical information, had been allowed to live. They would go on to establish law and order in this conquered kingdom, reshaping it into what it is today.

Chapter 23

The trainings were getting better each day and Ell,
the son of King Babul Ell, was reaching an
incredible level of power in battle; he even
surpassed his own master. The King needed to take
over the training of his son, to begin teaching him
his own fighting techniques. Ell's training
companion was a young boy, almost the same age,
who had been raised by the King and trained in the
same fashion as Ell. His name was Larey. Ell is
known as one of the strongest creatures in all Nede
Land, none compare to him in raw power or natural
talent. He is always accompanied by his best friend,
Larey. When you mention Ell's name, his shadow
arrives directly behind him in the sentence. *Larey.*
They are inseparable.

The skills of Ell were known to everyone; he was not
modest about showing his strength or challenging
even the strongest of opponents. In this way, Ell was
just like his father. As he grew, so did his training
capacity, passing from one master to another until
he had mastered the arts of every fighter in the
kingdom with exception, of course, of Babul Ell's
menacing fighting style. His father made sure not
only to teach him the great art of war that he had

learned from his master, but the arts he himself had perfected over years of experience as well.

....

As the King of one of the richest and largest lands in the kingdom, Babul Ell could not fight all the battles himself, there just wasn't time. Nor could he assign them all to his son, Ell or the fearless warrior, Larey. No, he needed to create an incredible force, or unit that could handle any and all possible threats to the kingdom without allowing it to escalate.

Thus, Babul Ell created the *Elite Guard Unit*. The King started recruiting young boys who were old enough to fight and carry weapons, training them in the ways of Babul Ell, creating the perfect and most deadly unit of soldiers imaginable. He placed them in charge of the security of the palace, and sent them out on patrols to keep a lookout for anything that could mean trouble for the kingdom. If there was something that threatened the peace and tranquility of the kingdom, it was the Elite Guard Unit's responsibility to handle it. Thus protected and at peace, the King focused himself on governing and training others in this way.

Since Babul Ell holds the most terrible and powerful secrets in Nede Land, some of which are known to other kingdoms while others are known only to him, an extra measure of security is needed. In case the day comes when the *worthy challenger* may appear to give the King the fight of his dreams.

King Babul Ell made sure that for anyone to challenge him to a fight, they must be worthy. He decreed that any challenger must undergo trials of escalating difficulty, and that they must pass every one in order to have the honor of challenging him.

. . . .

"First, I need to make sure that there can be no access to my kingdom from Earth. The treasures stored here must *remain* here. I care nothing for the safety or wellbeing of humanity. The treasures are the Holy Relics of my kingdom, and it will stay that way." Thought King Babul Ell.

"I must appoint someone worthy, someone who could never be defeated by anyone from this land, or from any other land for that matter. But it cannot be my son, I have a better and more challenging task for him. I have it! I will appoint Larey as the guardian of the gate to and from earth." Babul Ell was machinating and scheming, quite pleased with himself.

"He has the courage, the potential and the bravery to succeed at any task I give him. That's what I saw in him all those years ago. He is the finest and most tenacious warrior who ever lived."

He went swiftly to Larey to award him this great honor, taking long strides of confidence and joy. When he saw Larey, he smiled and took him by the shoulder.

"Larey, my son!"

"Father! It is good to see you. How may I serve my King this day?"

"I am glad you asked. Larey…" The King squeezed his son's shoulder and smiled even wider. "From this moment on, *you* will be the guardian of the gate to Earth. I can trust no one else with this great responsibility. None can enter this kingdom from Earth, and you are the only warrior capable of facing the array of intruders that may attempt to enter. You are free to walk across all the kingdoms of the earth and learn from them if you must; but do not mingle with or attach to their kind. You have already walked all the kingdoms of Nede Land, and I know you long for more, but there is nothing more important than this task." The King tempered his joy at his last remark, ensuring that Larey understood the gravity of the assignment.

Larey was about to speak and express his joy and humility, but the King stopped him.

"The time will come when someone will try to come to this kingdom from Earth, you cannot allow them to pass through the gate. The ancient books speak of a warrior that will come, but you are here to stop him and make sure he does not enter. Do you understand the burden I have placed on you? The great honor?"

"Yes, my king." Larey said with solemnity and grace. "Your will is my command."

"As I have shown you, there are great treasures in this kingdom, and if they fall into the wrong hands, I fear the worst. That is why I am entrusting you with this task. You are the pride of this kingdom and I am counting on you." With that, the great King dismissed his son to prepare for his task.

Chapter 24

"I must now call my son, Ell, and bestow upon him the greatest responsibility in the kingdom." The King summoned Ell to his presence, and he arrived quickly, as was his habit.

"Father! It is a joy to see you on this gorgeous day. How may I be of service?"

"How alike they are." Thought the King.

"My son, I have called you here today to give you a great and important task; the greatest task that I could possibly give."

Ell's face began to show his curiosity and anticipation.

"I know you've been curious about the content of the secret chambers, and today is the day I reveal them to you."

Ell was completely taken by surprise, but remained poised as not to ruin the dignity of his father's honor.

"Walk with me, and let us go to the secret chambers."

Father and son walked behind the stone wall to the rear of the throne room, through a secret door that was concealed there. Behind the door was a winding stairwell leading down, down into the bowels of the castle where Ell had never been. It was a long journey, so long that Ell thought they would fall out of the underbelly of the world before they reached the bottom. It became cold and dank like a cave, and his father's torch, which he'd lit at the beginning, began to flicker and wane. The King, seeing his son's concern, said,

"Not to worry, we are nearly there."

Shortly afterward, they arrived at the bottom. The passage widened into a moderately sized vestibule and the air became easier to breathe, restoring the torch. At one end of the wide room there was a door of stone flanked by two glittering blue torches.

"This is the secret treasure chamber. You've been here many times, but only when you were too young to remember. Now you and I are the only ones who know the location of this place. Let us enter the secret treasure chamber."

Ell had been struck silent by his father's revelation that he had taken him here as a boy. How could he not remember something so incredible?

Upon entering the chamber for the first time, Ell was surprised and amazed with the view. What an incredible display of powers, the most appealing of all being the swords, shining and roaring with energy. He felt as if they were speaking to him, so powerful were the irradiations of their might.

"What are those swords, father? And the incredible power coming from them! I have never felt anything like it before. Asked Ell in astonishment.

"These, my son, are the Holy Relics of this kingdom."

"I see there is a chamber for each one of them." Ell looked around and observed the structure of the room. "There are four chambers in each corner."

"Yes, my son. You are correct."

"But father, what about these towers passing through the center of each chamber, and what about that small chamber in the middle? I don't see any Holy Relic or sword in it." Continued Ell.

"My son, do not worry about the chamber in the middle, it is just for decoration. It has no meaning. *Your* job is to protect these four chambers," the King gestured around the room, "with your life. As well as the contents in each one of them."

"There is more than meets the eye in this chamber, and it will reveal things to you when the time comes. The legends speak of a warrior, as I have already told you, who is a worthy claimant of these Holy Relics and swords. He will be someone able to fight even me." For a moment, there was a somber heaviness in the air. Ell couldn't imagine someone strong enough to challenge his father. It didn't seem possible.

"You will need to defend the chamber and its contents at all costs, making sure no one gets their hands on them. Be aware, they have a life of their own." Ell looked with a sort of startled suspicion at the swords. "When their owner comes looking for them, they will awaken, and the results may be catastrophic to our kingdom. That is why you cannot allow anyone into this chamber."

Ell thought for a moment with his head down. "Father, you still have not told me what these powers and secrets are. I only see the Holy Relics, but I don't know what kind of power they have, even though I can sense a colossal and overwhelming presence in this place."

"It will all be revealed in time, just have some patience, my son." The King reassured.

"One last question for now, father. Did I see correctly, or was it just an illusion?"

"What do you mean by that, my son?"

"Well, I saw water running at the bottom of the chamber in the middle of the room."

The King smiled. "That is a mystery for another day, my son. You will understand in time. I am proud of you, as is every member of this kingdom. You are a true warrior, worthy to represent this kingdom anywhere. We are *Babul–Ell,* and we represent the gate of God."

....

As the guardian of the treasures in the Secret Chamber, Ell became the target for those who thought of themselves as the strongest. But Babul Ell knew what he had done. To entice other kingdoms, in a desperate search for the perfect fight, he created in his son a very, very appealing challenge for those who would seek to test their mettle, and spread the news all over Babul Ell Kingdom and greater Nede Land as well.

The reward was riches and gold, since it is the primary mineral in the kingdom, and a place in the palace. As if that was not enough, the King offered the hand of one of his daughters in marriage, which would secure for the winner the right to the throne. It was a difficult temptation to resist. Nevertheless, the reputation of Ell as the son of the greatest warrior in all Babul Ell Kingdom, and possibly in all Nede Land, was not something to be taken lightly.

Many have tried in the past, but none of them succeeded, which increased the reputation and legendary status of Ell as one of the strongest warriors in the kingdom. Even contenders with a thirst for greatness from the other kingdoms have tried and failed completely. It seemed like there was no match for King Babul Ell, his son Ell, or the peasant warrior Larey.

Larey is sometimes referred to as "the peasant warrior," because everyone knew he was not the son of the King, or of a royal blood. He has always been in the shadow of Ell. As the years passed by, Larey earned his own reputation fighting alongside Ell, proving to be worthy warrior. Some even say that the strength of Larey equals that of Ell. Some others have gone beyond this, saying that the Peasant Warrior's greatness is similar to that of King Babul Ell himself. Of course, these are only rumors and folklore from the people.

Chapter 25

While the team was reading God's Word, praying, and fasting, they felt something they were not accustomed to.

"Was that an Earthquake?" Asked Shrewder.

"I don't know, but I felt as if the floor was moving, and right after that there is the sound of something like the ringing of a bell. But I am not sure." Said Faith Woman.

The team felt it a second time, and they finally understood what was happening. The moment they had been waiting for had finally arrived and at the very same moment, their spiritual eyes were opened. They saw an immense gate opening for them to enter. The light coming from that door was blinding and incredibly terrifying, but they mastered their fear; their eyes were opened now and they could see better than ever.

"It is time, yes, it is time." They both said. "And our journey starts now."

. . . .

After emerging from the gate, they were welcomed by Larey in person.

"I have a message for you two. Perhaps I should call it a warning. You are entering one of the most dangerous kingdoms of this world, and not only that, but one of the strongest kingdoms as well. You have passed two stages of your training, but the third stage was not something you could endure on earth. However, this is not the time nor the place for your final trial, there is someone else already waiting for you. You have to understand that they will know that I have given you free passage and they will inquire as to the reason. That is why you went through your training, and you must demonstrate that you are strong enough to keep up with the challenges of the kingdom. That is the only explanation for your entrance into this kingdom. If you endure you first three trials, I will surely find the place and time to take you through your third stage of your training.

Larey stepped forward.

"For now, you may pass, but they are already waiting for you. Be strong and courageous, make me proud and show the potential I have seen in you!" Said Larey while departing. Finally, he turned and shouted in a gracious tone,

"Bonne Chance!"

. . . .

"Welcome to Babul Ell!" Said a man standing in the middle of the road. "I am *Ila* and I will be your opponent today. You must prove you are worthy to pass this post. For your information, there are three posts for you to pass and I am the luckiest for I am the first of your challengers. If, somehow, you manage to pass these three posts, the great Larey will welcome you at the fourth post, where he will decide your fate."

The challenger stepped forward and drew his sword, aggressively, but somehow gleefully.

"This is a kingdom of the strongest, and *only* the strong can walk this road. Do not disappoint me! I am sure, the great Larey saw something in you two and granted you passage because of it, because there is no way in heaven or in this world that you could defeat the great Larey."

Ila flourished his sword, drawing himself out of the reverie he'd been lulled into by the sound of his own voice.

"Shall we begin? Shall I fight the both of you at the same time, or one at a time?" He inquired.

Shrewder nodded in amusement. "While your welcome was warm and we appreciate the free information about the kingdom, there is no need for the both of us to fight, only one of us is enough at the moment." Faith Woman jumped into the conversation and said,

"Allow me the honor. After all, you always say that women should be first, correct?"

"Of course, I stand by my words!" Said Shrewder, laughing.

"I am Faith Woman and I will be your opponent today. Since you are asking for the strongest, I won't keep you waiting nor shall I hide my power from you. I will use my true strength from the beginning, as a gesture of appreciation."

At that moment, Faith Woman transformed into a totally different knight, with armor of emerald green and shimmering gold. Her helmet, diamond shield, and breastplate were all a radiant green and burnished bronze color. She was girded by a luminous silver belt from which hung a *Chokuto* sword, and she was shod with green Spartan's sandals.

"What a display of color and power." Commented Ila. "I am very glad we are starting on the right foot."

Shrewder leaned on a nearby tree growing on the edge of the road, and slid down into a seated position to enjoy the battle from a modest distance from the battlefield. He knew what was at stake, and he did not want to get involved in the fight, but just in case he stayed alert.

"Are you sure you don't want my help?" Shouted Shrewder.

"No, it is fine. I will be ok, just make sure you don't get in my way!" Faith Woman shouted above the din of the flames that surrounded her. "I wouldn't want to hurt you unwillingly." She turned to Ila and smiled.

"Are you ready, Ila?" She asked.

"Lets dance." He replied with relish.

....

"On a second thought," said Shrewder, rising from his spot under the tree, "I will go on ahead to the second post, since you don't need me here. I think we could save time that way. After all, we have a mission to accomplish."

Ila leapt in front of Shrewder in an attempt to stop him, but Faith Woman intervened. "Not so fast. Where do you think you are going" She chuckled. You are not allowed to move from here. *You* wanted to test my strength and now you'll get your wish. She charged him with a strong blow that forced him back to his previous position.

"You see, I have a very special sword." She held up the blade and it glinted in the sunlight. "Allow me to introduce you to her, she was made for cutting and thrusting. You should be honored to behold its might." Said Faith Woman, beaming with pride.

Pointing the tip of his sword in Faith Woman's direction, Ila stated "My sword's name is my name, we are one, and we have never been defeated. Prepare yourself for annihilation!"

With that, Ila rushed Faith Woman with terrific speed, creating a whirlwind behind him. He passed her with a swing of his razor-sharp blade, certain that he'd cut her deeply. But little did he know, *he* was the one who had received the blow. He turned to look back at his opponent, and fell to one knee.

"How?" He trailed off. Enraged, he lunged for again. This time he held nothing back, and once again believed he'd landed the blow. Yet again, he found that he had failed, and received another gash from Faith Woman's sword.

"I don't get it! What is happening? She is not attacking me, she is only blocking my swings and yet, I am the one bleeding." He was completely confused, and more bitter and angry than ever.

Faith Woman snapped her fingers saying, "Wake up, Ila! Don't overthinking it. Look, I'll enlighten you since this is not a fair fight. I don't *need* to attack you. When I use the back edge of my sword to deflect your attack, my precious sword reflects and magnifies the force of the blow, ensuring that the enemy is wounded, instead of me. As you can see, your attacks will not work on me. Now if I decide to attack you, then you will need to run for your life." Faith Woman laughed

"I see, so you think you're special!" Ila spat. "Allow me to show you my real strength!"

"Finally, I thought you were never going to take this seriously." Replied Faith Woman. Ila twirled around and initiated a downward vertical stroke with great force. He'd learned this time, however, and as Faith Woman deflected the attack rather easily, he saw the reflected energy and blocked it from hitting him. Simultaneously, he had lunged with his hidden tanto, cutting Faith Woman's forearm.

She licked the blood from her arm. "I like what I see now. Allow me to repay your kindness." She said with a bow and a grin. She took a few menacing steps forward and Ila seemed to cower in fear.

"What happened, my friend, are you scared of me? I thought you were looking for a strong rival." She was confused. "Don't be afraid, I don't bite. I *kill* but I don't bite." She laughed.

"You bloody woman! And I thought you were the decent type. You are enjoying this…" Ila was shaking attempting to maintain his composure. "You, you are just fooling around with me!" He summoned up the will to move his limbs, and in a blind panic of desperation, ran toward Faith Woman with all speed, attacking once again with full strength and both swords.

"I know your tricks now! I know how to beat you." He swung wildly, forcing her to block on the backstep. "Ha! Underestimate *me* will you! Get ready to go down, woman!" He was foaming at the mouth with fear and anger. Faith Woman threw him to the ground in disgust.

"What…happened?" Ila said softly from the ground. "It happened so fast, that I could not see…where did the hit come from?" He tried to replay it in his mind, he was able to see that, despite being in shock, she did not attack with her sword, but rather she kicked him squarely in his stomach.

Looking down at him, Faith Woman was partially obscured by the sun, appearing as a silhouette above him. "My name is not for decoration. I am not called "Faith Woman" for my beauty, it is because I received my faith from my master, and I have faith in my skills and strength; the strength that comes directly from Him." At this moment, Ila jumped up and swiped sloppily at her face in anger. She's had enough of this fool. She threw him over her shoulder and gave him a warning blow right above his eye which bled into his field of vision. But it was not the end for Ila, for he was a strong man. He was able to rush Faith Woman and return her blow, cutting her arm and kicking her across the field.

"You are not the only one who can play this game, I also have my style!" Said Ila charging once again with another of his deadly attacks. But it was too late. Faith Woman had decided to end him and his sniveling. She struck hard and with blinding speed at Ila's mid-section, hoping to leave him out of breath, but she decided she didn't care after he hit the ground. All she knew was that Shrewder was waiting for her. So she proceeded to the next outpost.

Chapter 26

From a short distance, but still concealed, someone was lurking in the bushes and watching the fight. He was having the best time of his life, enjoying a real fight and, most of all, being witness to the strength shown by Faith Woman.

Larey could not stand the thought of staying at Post Four, just waiting for them to arrive. He needed to witness firsthand the improvements his two pupils had made. After all, he was the one training them in the ways of Babul Ell Kingdom. "You are a strong woman, you really are. I am so proud of you, I just hope that you get to manage the two remaining guards for our next training." Whispered Larey to himself.

. . . .

"I am grateful, and I will always be so to King Babul Ell, for he is like a father to me." Larey pondered. "Maybe more than a father, since I do not recall anything about my real father, but what you have done is unforgivable."

He sat and speculated about the future.

"You must pay for what you have done to me and the pain you've caused, but I will not fight you myself. Since you are a father to me and your kingdom is my home, I must not allow myself to be consumed. I was there that night, father. I was hidden in the shadows. I saw you murder the one I loved, and I watched as you cursed my son. My sleepless nights of pain and sorrow all have a name, and that name is Babul Ell. I have suffered for years with the sickness of my son and with the absence of my love. I had to raise him alone!" He rose and shouted to the heavens in anguish and despair. "I have not even been able to tell him his true name, or what happened to his beloved mother!."

Larey sank to his knees in tears for moment, but gathered himself up, feeling the vengeance burning in his chest.

"It was you, King Babul Ell." He hissed the name. "Even though I cannot raise my hands against you, I will fulfil your dream and I will find the perfect warrior to bring you defeat. That is why I have trained Faith Woman and Shrewder, and the day has come for them to show me what they have learned. Your kingdom is at its end, and you will lose everything you hold dear, just as I have. I just wish that I could lay my hands on you myself, but I cannot raise my hands against my king and my father. I have tried to get rid of these feelings, but sometimes, I cannot contain them, and I know I will not be at peace until I bring my vengeance upon you for what you have done to me. I fight against these feelings, father, truly, but that is what I have in the depths of my heart, vengeance."

Previously, reports came to King Babul Ell that two uninvited guests were already in the kingdom.

"I am very glad to hear this. When Larey commented that he granted safe passage to two warriors, I was afraid he was joking, but now I see that he was deadly serious. What is he planning?" The King mused searchingly to himself.

"He mentioned that they are skilled fighters and worthy opponents. You have made my day with this news." He turned to the messenger and slapped him on the back, taking him off guard.

"Finally, some real action in this kingdom! It has been a long time since I've had any fun. I must experience these fights myself, and *before* I decide to engage them." Said the King to himself.

And so he decided to venture down to the Posts where they were fighting himself, and in disguise, to witness the fighters and analyze their styles, for, confident though he was in his own abilities, the King still harbored secret fears that he would be defeated. He arrived shortly thereafter, before the fight between Ila and Faith Woman took place. He was wrapped in a cloak and walking as though he were a decrepit wretch. He watched as Faith Woman sprung around the field like lightning, amazed at her speed and agility.

"I can see this woman has great style. It looks familiar somehow but I cannot decipher it. But I *like* it." Not only was the King in disguise, he was perched in a secret blind way up in a tree that bordered the road. He spent many free hours there, watching the road wistfully, hoping a worthy opponent would come down the dusty trail into his life.

"She has lied to Ila. She said that she is using her full strength, but that is not the case, she is only toying with him. I don't think he can defeat her, not even in her current state. I need to level up the game and make some changes at Post Two and Three if this is what is to be expected. I will need to bring my strongest fighters from the Elite Guard Unit." Thought the King. When the fight was over, he was filled with a mix of joy and astonishment. "This is going to be good."

"I will bring Bilat for Post Two, and just in case that man who came with his woman is able to defeat him, which I doubt, I will have Ramu on Post Three. There is no way they can defeat Ramu."

King Babul Ell could not see Larey and Larey could not see the King. They were enjoying the fight, but neither of them knew the other was present. By the time the King finished his scheming about reinforcing the Posts, Shrewder was walking up to Post Two. The guard on duty got up to approach the stranger, but his superior stopped him, directing him stand down.

Shrewder could see them chitchatting, but he was not able to hear a single word they said.

"I am Shrewder, and I come to challenge this Post. Let us not waste time and get this fight over with!" He shouted.

The guard on duty who had been conversing with his commanding officer turned sharply and waved to Shrewder, beckoning him closer.

"You must wait, the one who will fight you will be here shortly. Can I offer you something while you wait?" Asked the guard politely.

"What is he talking about?" Shrewder whispered to himself. "Look I am challenging you or whoever is on duty!" He shouted at the guard, then thought to himself "He's asking me if he can offer me something?" He thought for a moment. "I guess you can let me pass to the next Post." Both he and the guard laughed.

"I don't think that will be possible, but I can offer you some ale while you wait."

"Well, how can I refuse? After all, this is a new kingdom and what you are offering me should taste marvelous!" Added Shrewder with joy.

"Yes, it does! It is the best ale in the kingdom, or at least the best of the ale we guards are allowed to sip from time to time. Since you are a distinguished guest, I will share it with you."

For a moment, Shrewder felt very important, and thought to himself, "A distinguished guest, eh? What might that mean?" But he did not want to spoil the moment.

After a few glugs of the incredible and delicious ale, someone came out of the Post Station.

"I am glad you like our ale." The man said with a smile, dismissing the guard, who ducked away hurriedly. "And by the way, that was a good joke, asking to pass this post without a fight. You're funny, I'll give you that. I am Bilat, and I will be your opponent today."

Chapter 27

"What a good sense of humor this man has, I just hope his fighting is as good as his comedy." The King thought, chuckling softly.

Larey was watching as well, still unaware of his father's presence. Completely absorbed in watching Shrewder, he did not hear the almost imperceptible footsteps of someone trying to sneak up on him.

"Ha! Got ya! I knew you'd be too distracted to notice me!" Ell had crept up behind him and thrown his arm around Larey's neck, putting him in a choke hold. "You must be getting slow, brother!"

"Ell!" Larey shouted as the former let him go. The two embraced warmly.

"You beat me once again, brother." Said Larey.

"I heard the rumors and I knew you could not resist the temptation of watching the fights." Remarked Ell. "I'm sure father is somewhere here watching the fight as well. I could not waste the opportunity to watch the fight with my brother." Ell grabbed his brother's shoulder affectionately. "I really want to find out what you saw in them that inspired you to allow them into the kingdom."

Ell was not aware of Larey's intentions, and he had no idea of his traumatic experience with King Babul Ell. It was a secret Larey intended to keep for as long as he could.

"Well, you are late as always." Commented Larey, jokingly. "The first battle is already over. You see that women in armor?" He pointed to Faith Woman. "She has defeated Ila with no effort at all."

Ell's eyes went wide in disbelief. "You mean to tell me that the greenish armor girl defeated *Ila*."

"Just as I said, and she is now moving to meet her partner at the Second Post. I think we should move a little further to catch next fight. You will see for yourself the treasure I have found for you, brother." Said Larey in a joyful tone of voice.

"But wait a minute, who is guarding your post while you are out here, Larey?"

"That is not something you need to worry about, I got it covered. Besides, who would be dumb enough to attempt fighting me after all this time?" They both laughed with relief.

. . . .

"Nice to meet you, Bilat. I am Shrewder, and I thank you for coming to my assistance." Said Shrewder, smiling.

"Assistance? You must be joking. Don't confuse hospitality with innocence. I am not here to assist you in any way, I am here to defeat you." Chastised Bilat.

"I must disagree with you. You see, you are already assisting me by showing up, and offering yourself for defeat here today. Once I defeat you, I will just move to the next post." Bilat grew anger at this cavalier treatment. "That is." Shrewder continued, "if my companion does not get there before I beat you. You are just a means to an end." He smiled.

"What a confident man you are." Bilat spread his feet into a fighting stance. "Let us see if you can back up your words."

. . . .

Bilat is one of the top elites in the Elite Guard Unit, and has been trained by Babul Ell himself. He has never lost a fight and is the next fighter from the Babul Ell to fight in the *Soultai* Tournament in Hont Well.

King Babul Ell selects the best fighters to participate in an elimination contest, to earn the right to participate in the Soultai Tournament. Only the top two fighters receive this great honor.

First, the candidate must fight his training partners and defeat them. Then, he needs to fight his previous masters for approval, testing their strength and endurance against seasoned instructors. Once he has gained approval of his previous masters, he is eligible to receive additional training from King Babul Ell, and it is only after the candidate has mastered the ultimate training of the King that he is worthy of calling himself the next Soultai fighter.

The King makes sure that the candidate is not emotionally attached to his life on Babul Ell, because once this champion wins the championship tournament, he will no longer be part of Babul Ell Kingdom, rather he will become a new citizen of Hont Well. There is prestige, honor, glory and power, among other benefits, for the kingdom that produces a winner. It is a privilege to send such strong fighters to participate in the tournament, and all hope that their contender will become the pride of Nede Land.

. . . .

Not more talk, show me what you got!" Said Bilat.

"You took the words out of my mouth!" Shouted Shrewder, jumping into the air and sending his first blow crashing down on Bilat, hurting slightly.

"Just a scratch! I thought your blow was going to be stronger." Teased Bilat.

"Don't worry about it, my friend. I was only unsheathing my Aikuchi Katana sword. That scratch wasn't even caused by an attack!" Responded Shrewder. "Allow me to show you what a real attack looks like!" At that moment, Shrewder unleashed a powerful attack of white and blue flames, distracting Bilat. Through the storm of fire Shrewder swung his sword and cut Bilat's leg. The sight was spectacular. The blow was not fatal, because Bilat was able to block it partially; but the mere shockwave of the mighty attack wounded him.

"I thought you would be one of the strongest opponents." Shrewder mocked. "Why don't you attack me, and I will not attack you in return." He sheathed his sword once more and stood perfectly still.

"Let us do something. I will give you the opportunity to give me your best two strikes. I will not attack; you have my word. But in return, I get to unleash one attack against you. What do you think? Do we have a deal or are you too afraid to indulge me?" Smirked Shrewder.

Picking himself up and dusting himself off, Bilat replied, "I agree to your challenge."

Meanwhile Larey and Ell were still watching the fight, and Ell leaned over to Larey, sating "What a dumb decision, it is obviously a trap. He will not be able to survive one full attack from the strange fighter and I know he is not even using his full strength."

"His name is Shrewder, or that is what his friends call him. He is one of the strongest from his group, but he does not like to show his real strength. I had some trouble getting him to relax and show his full strength, and in the end, he always held back; like he was afraid of something." Added Larey.

"I see." Said Ell, looking back at Shrewder. "I understand why you chose him now, I think. He is *worthy*. And I can say that the greenish woman is also worthy."

"Her name is Faith Woman, and even though she is not among the strongest, she does not know her full strength. She has an incredible and dauntless power hiding inside her." Commented Larey.

King Babul Ell was also watching the fight from a distance and he already knew the outcome of the battle.

"I am sorry Bilat, I was not aware of the strength of this warrior. if I had known it, I would not have put you in this situation. You are risking your life and you don't even know it." Thought the King to himself. "Either way, I am glad to see this fighter."

The King was not done with his train of thought, when Bilat sent his first successful blow into Shrewder, sending him skidding on his heels several yards from the force. A couple of feet with the blow. Without hesitation, as he was a clever warrior who knew to capitalize on his success, Bilat followed up this attack with another, more powerful technique, aiming to finish before he wore out. This sent

Shrewder to one knee, apparently affected by the combo.

"I knew you couldn't resist," Shrewder smiled with a trickle of blood running down his cheek. "but you've made a big mistake, my friend. Allow me to enlighten you. The reason why I offered you the strike exchange is because I did not want to force the battle, I wanted to finish it without complication and, most of all, I am not ready to show my real strength. Those who are watching!" He shouted knowingly, "will need to wait to see me get real." Added Shrewder.

"What are you talking about? It is only you and me, there is no one else around." Said Bilat confusedly.

"You are mistaken, but it does not matter. Say your last words." Shrewder did not want to take Bilat's life, and so decided to rush him with a fraction of his strength, which was more than enough to end the fight. In a whirl of power and energy, Shrewder crushed Bilat's armor and knocked him unconscious with the pressure of the air alone. "It is done."

Chapter 28

"What a considerate man. He is really a strong opponent. He did not want to take the life of his opponent." Thought the King to himself. "I want to see more, I want to provoke the true potential and power of this man. I think that I will be able to see it at the next post. He will face Ramu and that will be a fight to see."

"Well, your Shrewder guy is a passionate and strong fighter indeed. I just don't understand why he pitied his rival." Said Ell. "Obviously, he is way stronger than Bilat, so he should have just finished him for good." He added.

"That is Shrewder for you. He can control his emotions and feelings and at the same time show mercy to his opponent. What an incredible display of splendor." Replied Larey.

"It sounds like you know a lot about him and you are proud of him as well, little brother." Mentioned Ell with a tinge of irony. Larey did not bother to answer his brother's sarcasm.

"Should we go to Post Three and watch Ramu fight? Faith Woman or Shrewder?" Asked Larey.

"Sure, let us go." And they departed.

. . . .

"Your majesty, Ramu has surpassed all his mates in strength and tactical prowess. I believe he is a great candidate for taking over key positions in the kingdom." The King's Advisor bowed with his last word and stepped back with deference and respect.

The King nodded knowingly and contemplatively. "Bring Ramu to me and we will see how strong he is."

When Ramu came to the king, he appeared pleased to see him. A very tall man with a body shaped by and *for* battle, with rippling muscles undulating underneath the cloth of his tunic. The pressure coming from Ramu was immense, and clearly demonstrated the magnitude of his fighting ability. The King was tempted to exchange a few blows with Ramu, to test if his instincts and the reports from his advisors were correct, but he resisted the temptation. He leaned forward in his chair and indicated that Ramu should speak.

"From what part of the kingdom do you hail, Ramu?" He asked.

"Your Majesty, I am from a small tribe that is situated along the southeast border of Mock Fenk Fist Kingdom. We are one of the few towns in the kingdom where training begins in childhood. Every child who is worthy strives to master the art of fighting. Every sinew in my body has been hardened by the most intense competition; it made me the man I am today."

The King nodded with approval and fascination. Ramu continued, his pride getting the better of him for a moment.

"I have defeated opponents of all types from around the kingdoms. I have been training to serve you, my king. I pledge my strength and my life to you!"

At this moment, Ell was walking through the corridor adjacent to the audience chamber, on his way to see his father. Babul Ell looked directly into Ramu's eyes.

"Attack the first person who enters this hall." Ramu cocked his eyebrow up as if his mind were attempting to process what he'd just heard.

"Show no mercy, and do not stop until I command you to do so."

The huge oak doors of the chamber opened, and Ell stepped through, dressed in fine clothing and wearing a smile that matched. Ramu whirled around and instantly launched into the air, plunging downward with all his strength in a windmill kick. Ell, though taken by surprise, easily blocked the attack, locking Ramu's leg for a moment

"I don't know who you are or why you're attacking me, but if it's fun you want, it's fun you'll have." Ell said with a devilish grin.

The two bounded away from one another and initiated a fierce duel. Each man utilizing a creative range of styles back to back, changing to match the onslaught of the other. They were both skilled and versatile fighters, and the King wanted to know if Ramu could keep up with his son. He saw that neither was using his full strength, despite the fact that the King told Ramu specifically to show no mercy.

"Interesting. Stop!" Commanded the King. And after a final lightning quick exchange, the two halted and turned to kneel before the king, like glorious actors upon a stage who had just finished a performance.

"You are strong and you fight well." Said the King. "My son, what do you think of him?"

"He is strong, my King. I am glad to have him as a friend, and not as an enemy."

"Haha! Indeed!" And all in the chamber laughed together. That was the beginning of Ramu's legend; the man who fought the mighty Ell to prove his worth to the great King Babul.

The King sent specific instructions to Ramu before he encountered his target at Post Three. The message, which bore the royal seal, was as follows:

"The Kingdom of Babul Ell is known to be strong in faith. The people have tremendous faith in their King, and this faith is one of the greatest aspects of the kingdom. We always show restraint and a refined ability to discern truth from falsehood. In fact, some might even call this the kingdom of miracles.

The way I, King Babul Ell, conduct this kingdom, bringing richness and peace to all citizens, is a miracle in itself. We are the head of the Malsi Group and you must prevail, that our dignity might remain intact. Do not hold back, and do not lose this battle. I am proud of you and your strength, but it is time for you to show me your true potential. I will be watching your fight."

Chapter 29

"What took you so long?" Asked Shrewder.

"Well, the distance between Posts One and Three is greater than I anticipated." Said Faith Woman, catching her breath.

"Any problem with your rival at Post One?"

"Nope. No problems at all. I hurried to meet you at Post Two but you were not there anymore. I saw the signs of battle, but nothing else. I immediately knew you were heading for Post Three. I am glad we made it here." Faith Woman placed her hand on Shrewder's shoulder in a gesture of warmth and satisfaction.

"My adrenaline is pumping now and I need a fight." She bit her bottom lip with anticipation, practically begging to fight. "So?"

"So what?" Shrewder replied.

"So can I have this one, please?" Faith Woman said, completely breaking down, wringing her hands together in supplication.

Shrewder rolled his eyes. "Well how can I reject

such a *polite* request from you, madam?" And he bowed low, sweeping his hand through his waist.

"Yay!" Faith Woman exclaimed.

"We need to get our training through with soon, I sensed a presence looking on from a distance and the power was immense. We need to rise to the level of these gigantic powers I have been feeling." Commented Shrewder.

"Yes," Faith Woman said, rising from the ground where she'd been begging and looking off into the distance. "I have sensed that too." She screamed into the wind, "Is there anyone here! Who is the lucky one that gets to fight me today?"

After the echoes of her shouts died away, they heard a faint but steadily increasing sound, like that of a great beast treading its way across the landscape.

"Look!" Shrewder pointed to a spot in the distance.

There, coming through the blurry heat radiating off the ground in the noon-day sun, was some terrifying behemoth of a man. He seemed to lumber rather than walk, and his arms and legs swung along like loose tree trunks locked to a mass of moving flesh. Neither of them could believe their eyes for a moment, but the moment passed quickly as he drew ever nearer, and surprising quickness for something so gargantuan. The full terror presented itself with a lurching grunt, stopping a few yards away from where they stood.

Faith Woman, now recovered from the shock, closed her gaping mouth and shouted, "YOU are a huge man!" She turned to Shrewder and made threw her thumb in the giant's direction, as if to say "Get a load of this guy!" She walked up to him, and looked at his face as one does when gazing up at a tall sky-scraper, almost falling over. Fearlessly, she said in a low voice "The good news is, the bigger you are, the harder you fall."

The great hulk was implacable, and silent.

"Well," she muttered, cracking her knuckles, "I assume you are the one to fight me, so I will not waste any time. I'm hyper, and I need to release this power inside me or I'm going to explode!" With that she unleashed an incredible punch, planting it directly in his navel. The shockwave cracked the ground and blew the leaves from the tree directly behind them.

The gigantic man, however, was unphased. Faith Woman back flipped and landed a few feet away. "Man!" She shouted. "It's like hitting a brick wall." She shook her fist and readied herself for another attack. "This'll be good."

The titan merely stared off into the distance, allowing the dust and dirt from the blast of Faith Woman's punch to settle gently upon his face and shoulders. Faith Woman leapt at him once more and drove another punch into his face, initiating a flurry of attacks that blurred the air and scorched the dust off the man's face. She drew back her right arm, and gathered all her strength for another punch, and then let loose with a finishing move that lit her hand with red flames. The blast from the punch choked the air with black smoke as she hopped back to survey the damage.

"Got ya." She said with confidence.

The smoke began to clear, and the smile gradually faded from her face as she realized that not only was her opponent still standing, he was as unmoved as before.

"What the…seriously???"

"I am Ramu," the man boomed with a deadly calm yet unnerving voice, "and you are no match for me."

Before she could even think, Faith Woman felt a pain in her stomach that almost made her faint. Ramu had kicked her square in the belly, and she hadn't even seen him move. But she did hear her ribs splitting. The force propelled her across the field, and sent her rolling to Shrewder's feet.

"Are you sure you don't need help?" He asked, looking down at her.

"I…I'm fine." She gasped. She pushed herself back up with an effort, spat a streak of blood on the dirt, and clenched her fists.

"All right, no more games."

This time, with a deep breath, her strength increased ten-fold, and an incredible fire burst from her Spartan sandals. There was a low hum emanating from her now, and that hum intensified as she drew her sword.

Ramu's eyes seemed to flash when she drew the sword, but they became icy and unchanging once more a fraction of a second later. Faith Woman began to levitate, and with a tap of her foot on the ground, flew straight toward Ramu with blazing speed. She struck him directly on the shoulder with her blade, caving him to his knee.

"I cannot exchange blows with you," she gasped as she realized the fight she was in for, "and strength is not going to help me much either. But I have something even better to take you down."

"Oh, what is that, woman?" Inquired Ramu, returning to his feet.

"I have my faith and I have *this*." She charged him once again, increasing her strength even more. This blow landed in his solar plexus, and it was so hard that she flew off his body and smashed into the dirt, hard, almost completely exhausted. Ramu sank to both knees, but otherwise remained unperturbed.

"No one but my masters have been able to make me bend the knee. You are indeed strong, woman." He rose to his feet again. "I don't understand where your strength is coming from, but you will need more of it to defeat me." For the first time, Ramu moved from where he'd been standing. He took two enormous strides and drew his sword from its scabbard and swung a downward blow at Faith Woman in one motion. She raised her sword to deflect it, but as his blade made contact with her Chokuto, it gave way and split in two. Faith Woman winced, and almost in slow motion she made peace with God; this was the end.

Ramu's sword halted, an inch in front of her face. She sheepishly opened one eye, then the other, to find that Shrewder's sword had solidly stopped the mighty Ramu's blade from cleaving her in two. Now, both men were staring at one another with curiosity.

"Not so fast, she is my friend and I cannot allow you to hurt her." With a flick of his wrist, Shrewder flung Ramu's sword to the side, giving him just enough time to whisk Faith Woman aside to safety. He put her down gently and, with a smile said "It is ok, you rest now, I will take care of it."

Shrewder turned away from her and immediately sent his first attack toward Ramu. It was a shockwave from his sword that was meant to distract, and it worked. In the split second it took Ramu to blink, Shrewder had already crossed the field and initiated his second attack. Ramu was truly taken by surprise, and when he raised his sword to defend himself, he could not summon the strength to effectively guard, and Shrewder's mighty blow plowed through his defense, slicing a thin crimson line across Ramu's chest. Shrewder's sword hit the ground and the force that was translated into it produced an earthquake that caused Ramu to falter and kneel a *third* time.

Ramu tried to counterattack, but he was short of breath this time. His opponent was on a different level, he knew that now. He managed to get back on his feet, but there was already another blow coming down upon him, and he watched in slow motion as the shining blade slashed his leg. Shrewder was not kidding around.

"I cannot lose this battle; I must make my king proud." Thought Ramu. At that moment, inspired with renewed pride for his king, Ramu released his brutal and awesome power in the form of an incredible swing of his sword which struck Shrewder's guard, flinging his sword to the wayside.

Shrewder looked briefly at the weapon hurtling through the air, and made the fateful decision to unleash his true power. A flaming "3" appeared on the upper portion of his right breast, and his clothing flashed in a brilliant display, revealing his impressive physique, wreathed in flame and his sandals changed from a leather material to that of crimson dragon scales. The fire increased in intensity as he took a few steps closer to Ramu.

"Impossible." Ramu whispered in disbelief.

Shrewder disappeared in a hurricane of fire and burning dust that consumed Ramu completely. The wind stung his face and arms, and in this dizzying hurricane the only thing he could register was the pain of a thousand slashes appearing all over his leathery body. He desperately tried to gather his thoughts as he swung his sword into the cyclone. He didn't know what was happening, but he knew he was bleeding, badly.

Chapter 30

"What an incredible speed! What power! I feel, I feel… I don't know. I feel happy." Thought the King while watching the fight. "This guy's incredible and it is a mystery where his power is coming from. I want to see more." He laughed with an evil tone.

"Red sandals with fire? Number 3 on his chest?" Even though Ell and Larey were at distance, they were able to see the red sandals and the number on Shrewder's chest.

"What does this number mean? Where is the fire coming from?" Asked Ell of Larey in a surprised tone of voice.

"I don't know, I have never seen this before. I mean, I have seen the sandals, but not the fire nor the red color that looks like fire, and I have no idea what that number means either. This is totally new to me as well." Replied Larey.

"Well, Ramu. I know you are not using your full power." Shrewder had dissipated the hurricane and floated back down to the earth. "Show me your true colors." He said. Ramu was regaining his balance. He looked over at the flaming knight and decided it wasn't worth holding back any longer. He spread his legs and clenched his fists at his hips, using a concentration technique the King had taught him. Shrewder felt his power increase dramatically.

"Let's see you toy with me now." Ramu sneered. He crushed his feet into the ground and propelled himself at Shrewder with a sonic boom. He punched Shrewder with a devastating blow on the jaw.

A few drops of blood fell to the ground from Shrewder's lips. "Now that is something. I didn't even know I could still bleed." Shrewder said slyly as he wiped the blood from his face.

"You are a strong fellow, I will need to level up too." Shrewder emanated a wave of red flames that began to encircle Ramu. About Shrewder's waist, a silvery belt with a red flicker appeared.

"A belt, what is he going to do with a belt?" Thought the King from a distance. "How many more tricks can this man have?"

From behind, Shrewder heard a voice. "Can you stop fooling around with this man? End this fight now." Shrewder looked over his shoulder and winked at Faith Woman.

Ramu began to levitate, the flames did not burn him, and were almost relaxing. He was mesmerized somewhat, not knowing exactly how to respond, but he did suspect that he could no longer contend with the man in front of him.

"There was never any hope you could win, Ramu. The Lord decided your fate long ago." And with that, Shrewder appeared beside Ramu and engulfed him in the growing fire storm. As he disappeared, as though he were drowning in his own defeat, the King felt that he'd betrayed Ramu. The two opponents vanished for a moment, and when they reappeared, the fight was over.

....

"Who is this man and where is this power coming from? I feel an overwhelming power coming from him." Mentioned Ell. "I must go see my father and find out why it's so important for these two to be here. I will catch up with you later, Larey."

"Sure, no problem." Larey responded. He was focused on the fruit of his training. "I want to see what will happen when he completes the third stage. If this is what he's capable of at only stage two, imagine…"

....

"Father, you have not yet told me what it is that we are keeping in the secret chamber of treasures. I would like to know because this man is coming to claim it and I still don't know what he is after or what I am guarding at my post." Stated Ell Emphatically.

The King rose from his seat. "Throughout the history of the human race, there have been Gifts bestowed upon humans; these gifts live among them, grow in strength, control nature and beasts and learn to live with one another. But once, an especially smart spirit confused them and brought chaos into them. This scattered the Holy Relics all across earth. They are so powerful that humans could defeat us without any problem at all, and their hearts would be content. This is why we needed to step into existence, otherwise the existence of the relics would not make sense at all. There are two types of Holy Relics, and though sometimes they share names, their powers and essences are not the same. These are to be held by humans only because they were made for them. We can only hide them or keep them, and our power does not come from them. But from time to time, we feel the essence of these Holy Relics and their waves spreading out and calling to humans. Then, we become tarnished with part of this power. One group is called "gifts" and the other is called "fruits.""

"You must never confuse them; the first ones are pure strength and power. In ancient times, these were the only ones available to humanity, but then the one they call *Savior* appeared, and afterward the second group showed up and was made available to them. It is said that those who possess the second group, are not bound by any law in nature or in spirit. In Babul Ell Kingdom we have been holding four Holy Relics since ancient times, keeping them from humanity. We are holding two from the group of Gifts, named "*Discernment and Miracles.*" And from the group of *Fruit*, we are holding two more, called "*Belief and Control.*" Or, as they call them, "*Faith and Temperance.*"

"We must protect them at any cost. We could afford to lose the two Relics from the first group, but the ones from the second group are uncontrollable, deadly, and powerful beyond your imagination. A warrior possessing them would be invincible. Not even I could defeat him. If we have to fight them, we must try to fight them by the water. We cannot afford to lose under any circumstances! This man, I have seen it, his strength is almost comparable to mine and I am sure he has been withholding his real strength."

"Father, but why by the water? You mean by Posin river?"

"Yes, there is a secret in Posin river. According to the legends and ancient books, if any human gets into Posin river, whoever it is, because it is human, his power will vanish as long as he is touching the water. The origin of Posin and its power is another mystery only known to me, and now I pass them to you, my son."

"Father, how many more secrets do we have in Babul Ell Kingdom?" Asked Ell, stupefied.

"Too many my son, too many." Said the King, laughing. "This is Nede Land, my boy. One day you will understand."

Chapter 31

"They have defeated three of my warriors, according to the rules they are entitled to spend a few days in the kingdom, but I will have Larey keep an eye on them to make sure they don't get any stronger." Thought the King to himself.

"Larey, I have summoned you because I need you to be the guardian of the two foreigners for the next 10 days, as is customary. Whatever you do, don't leave their side. I don't want them to get any stronger. I will think of how to deal with them in time."

"Yes, my king, your wish is my command." Responded Larey, dutifully.

"He has no idea that I am the one training them, or that they are here because of me. I thought it was going to be difficult to train them, but the King has made it possible."

. . . .

"You are finally here! I am very glad you've made it. I am quite impressed with your power. I have seen moves I did not know you had!" Larey said, tapping Shrewder on the shoulder. "Faith Woman, you have shown a faith worthy of your name and you have survived, which is one of the most important things in battle. Do not feel ashamed or discouraged because there was someone stronger than you, there is always someone stronger out there, even when we think we are the strongest ones!" Comforted Larey.

"By the will of the King, I am your guardian. It is a great advantage because I have been instructed not to leave your side for any reason, not even for a moment. This is the perfect excuse to train you. I was having a hard time thinking of a way to complete your training here, but the King, without knowing it, made it possible. Let us be grateful." Continued Larey with glee.

"Now, allow me to enlighten you. The reason why the third stage of your training was not possible to complete it on earth, is because there are limitations there, and it is impossible to reach your full potential without causing damage to the Earth. Of course, this training will be a little different than before. I may need to release my full power as well and that is something I don't want anyone to feel. Shrewder and Faith Woman were attentively listening to every word coming out of Larey's mouth.

"C'mon, follow me, we will go to my private place." Larey seemed to be giving them a tour, showing them where they were going to be sleeping during their short stay in Babul Ell Kingdom. He seemed proud of his land, despite his hidden hatred for the King.

"The accommodations are not first class, but this is a royal chamber for guests to stay." He gestured to the apartment they found themselves walking into.

"Wow! A royal chamber!" Exclaimed Faith Woman. "I am staying in a royal chamber. Who would have thought that I would ever be in a place like this."

When they arrived at the end of the chamber, there was a little inscription on the wall, something they did not understand. Larey reached out with his hand and touched the inscription. A secret door appeared from out of the stone, thus giving them access to another chamber entirely. This is my secret training and hiding spot. No one in the kingdom knows about it. It took me many years to build it myself, and it was especially difficult to do in secret. I created this place as my training center because I never wanted others to notice my real power and potential; I have been hiding it from the King and Ell. Until today they had never seen my real power." Somehow there was a melancholic tone in Larey's voice.

He decided to tell them the real reason he was helping them. He told them about his adventure and the love of his life. He told them the sad tale of what the king did to her and his son, who was now growing up without a mother because of the king's actions. Now they felt a bit of remorse and anger in his words.

"I had to hide my own son so he could survive." He explained to them the sickness that befell his boy, and explained his location on earth.

A single tear rolled down his perfect face, but when he looked back Faith Woman and Shrewder were crying alongside him, so moved where they by his tale.

"Don't worry, we got you covered, Larey." Shrewder said while Faith Woman pat him on the shoulder. "The One we serve is greater than any enemy; we serve the Lord Almighty, Elohim, God of all creation."

. . . .

The training was going well, and the team seemed to be catching up; after all, they did not have much time, so, they needed to train day and night.

"What is happening, are you distracted?" Inquired Larey. "It is about time for you to understand and master the final phase of your training if you want to survive what is coming." He was deadly serious, and the team could feel his intensity in the way he was pushing them beyond their limits. A few more days passed, and the team remained in the heat of training. Larey, surveying them and judging their movements, walked around the outer rim of the training den.

"There is just one day left of your training! Tomorrow the King will have your next opponents ready and believe me, whoever he chooses is not going to be an easy to defeat!" He spoke with fervor and energy. "That is if Ell does not convince the King that *he* should fight you instead."

"That is music to my ears!" Said Faith Woman. To which Shrewder added, "I don't think that I will like this kind of music."

"You still don't understand, if Ell joins the fight, there is no way you can beat him in your current state." Larey said looking at Shrewder with seriousness. "He will want to fight you and he will use you as a training bag; his power is beyond your imagination. I have been training with that man since we were six and I have never seen anything like his strength, and to make matters worse, he is just like his father in temperament." He lowered his head with a look of contemplativeness on his face. "I don't think the King will get involved, because he would need to be challenged to enter into a fight, but if the King decides to use you as target practice, my purpose will have been in vein." He concluded in a forlorn and helpless tone.

"Observe and learn. As you can see there is *joy* in my movements, and a combination of **peace** and *love* in my every blow. As I have told you before, it is not simply about fighting, you need to find peace, joy and love in your fighting style. You need to master these three last elements before you can release your full power. Allow me to show you."

Larey took a step back and assumed a meditative stance. He took a deep breath inward, and as he exhaled, he released approximately eighty five percent of his power into the atmosphere. The pressure was so profound and overwhelming that it nearly made them cry with unexplainable emotion. Immediately he decreased the level of his power. They felt as if the room was going to implode with the immense power coming from Larey, but they had to gird themselves up and stand strong so that they were not blown away completely.

"Finally," Larey whispered as he opened his eyes and breathed deeply once more, "you are able to master the final three elements, but our time is up. You will face your fate in an hour according to the King's wish. I hope you'll be able to break the seal holding you back and unleash your true power, otherwise, I fear the worst."

"We will succeed in His name." Said Faith Woman and Shrewder.

"There is something else I have not told you; I was hoping for you to discover it on your own, but time is of the essence. The passage of time in this world is not the same as in your world.

Time here is a matter of perspective and it can run a thousand times slower than in your world. And the laws of gravity are different as well, but I think you've managed to understand that already. Just a piece of advice to you two: Make me proud." The training was over, but Shrewder and Faith Woman were still not yet able to unleash their maximum power.

Chapter 32

"I hope you've enjoyed the hospitality of my kingdom and the plenitude of its resources in the last ten days. That period of rest is customarily afforded the winner of a good fight. Today, I will decide your fate! Your very lives are in my hands and I will be swift and terrible in judgment." Larey, Ell and all the members of the Elite Guard Unit were present, as were other high officials of the kingdom.

The King continued after a pause.

"We are a fair kingdom and we believe that the strong will always prevail. After watching your strength, I have decided that only one of you will fight my next opponent. The woman," the King pointed to Faith Woman and paused. All gathered, including Shrewder and Ell held their breath, "will no longer fight. Only the man will be allowed to fight as this is a fight for the stronger of the two and she has a long way to go still. But you," pointing at Shrewder, "you are something else. I am eager to see your true colors."

Faith Woman made a motion as if she was about to speak against the King's will, but Shrewder told her not to do so. "It is ok, I will handle it." He said, gently. "Don't worry." Faith Woman decided to listen to her partner. She knew somehow, deep in her heart, that she was not yet ready for this league of fighting.

"Honorable king," Shrewder projected as he stood to address the King, "if I may be allowed to speak."

"Please, go ahead." Insisted the king.

"My partner has been disqualified without a fight, and that is acceptable, but I think it would be fair to grant her one wish. After all, she has already defeated one of your warriors."

The King paused and thought for a moment, and Shrewder interrupted with another request. "And the terms, what are the terms if I win the next battle?"

Amused, the King asked, "Do you have any more requests or conditions before the fight?"

"I do not."

"Very well then, your partner may have a wish and I will make sure her wish is granted. As for you, what is it that you desired the most?" Asked the King.

"If I win, I want access to your Secret Chamber, and I want to retrieve two of the Holy Relics. That is the reason for my fight and that is want I want the most." Shrewder stated defiantly.

"Very well then," said the King, "I will grant your wish. If you defeat my fighter, your wish will be your reward."

At that moment, the King stood up and yelled across the stadium, "Larey!" When, Faith Woman and Shrewder heard that name, they trembled in the inmost depths of their minds.

"It cannot be him, it cannot be Larey! There is no way I can defeat *him*." Thought Shrewder for a moment. Then, resolved to fight honorably no matter the outcome, he lowered his head and smiled. "If this is it, I'm going down fighting."

"I cannot be the one to fight him, he is not ready. Blast!" This was one among the many thoughts that were passing through Larey's mind until the King's words broke his frenzied trance.

"Make room for my son! Ell will be the one to fight them."

Confused but relieved, Larey looked with a start toward the center of the arena and saw Ell walking haughtily, waiving to the crowd. They all cheered uproariously for him. "I don't know whether to be relieved or even more worried for Shrewder. I fear the worst."

Meanwhile, Shrewder was thinking about the stories he'd heard of Ell. He was a legendary man, and an almost invincible fighter whom no one had ever defeated; this would surely prove to be a once in a lifetime battle.

"Fate had brought the two of you together. You've got this." Reassured Faith Woman, patting Shrewder on the back as he turned to face Ell.

"You will fight Ell because he is the guardian of the Secret Chamber; if you defeat him, he will grant your wish. You will also receive the honor and privilege that comes with winning a fight like this. You will be betrothed to one of my daughters, and receive richness and wealth beyond your dreams. But," the King raised a finger as if to more forcefully illustrate the next point, "beware, all who have come before you have perished trying to defeat my son." He glowered down at Shrewder as he finished this last sentence.

"Your highness, fulfilling my wish would be more than enough to satisfy me, but since your generosity is beyond imagination and you are a fair king, I would ask nothing more than free passage back to our world." Added Shrewder.

"That is for Ell to decide, if you manage to survive."

. . . .

Ell's confidence in his own power and strength was one of a kind, for he knew the maximum capability of every fiber of muscle that wound its way around his entire body. All his adventures had taught him the value of patience and endurance, and, consequently, he learned to master his senses and force them to do his bidding whenever he called upon them. Most warriors fight and give their lives for a leader or an ideal of some kind, but Ell's only purpose had been to find a worthy opponent to fight with, just like his father.

"This is Babul Ell!" The son of the King boomed from the arena and gestured in a grand sweep at his father. "and I am Ell, the prince of this Kingdom!" The crowd went wild and stood to honor the Prince. "I am proud and I am thrilled that today we have before us a man whom my father has deemed worthy of my sword!" Amid the furor of the crowds ecstatic cheering, Ell turned away, whispering to himself, "But not worthy enough to win."

Lowering his hands to signal that he wanted quiet, Ell spoke once more. "I will show my appreciation for this warrior! If he can hold his ground against me for 10 minutes, I will grant him his wish regardless," the crowd gasped. "but access to only ONE Holy Relic. If he is able to *defeat* me, well…" he laughed softly, "Then he may have access to the Secret Chambers and all that is stored therein."

The King was speechless as he listened to this declaration, but it was the Prince's declaration, and as such, he was required to honor and support it; after all, he was sure that the fighter would prove to be no greater threat than a punching bag. Nonetheless, the King wanted to see how strong this man was and there was no one better way than to have his own son, the second strongest on their world, provoke and antagonize him.

Chapter 33

The palace was in a commotion with the news that Ell himself would be fighting the strange visitors. Every challenger to the guardian of the Chamber of the Secret Treasures had fought in the open field, or, when a challenge was announced in enough time, in the coliseum. This time, the fight was going to take place in the palace, and there was not enough space for all the people to fit in.

The daughters of the King were very happy to be watching the great warriors that were about to fight. After all, there was the possibility that one of them would be engaged by the end, and that excited them almost beyond words.

"What is this noise and this commotion outside?" Said the King "Send the Elite Unit Guards to check that out at once." After a brief wait, the Captain of the Guard returned with news. He snapped to the King's side and saluted.

"My king, the people have gathered, they are demanding to watch the fight as they have done in the past. They want to see their Prince fight."

The King, mildly annoyed but pleased that his people had such pride in his son, paused for a moment. "Very well then, go and inform them that we will have the fight in the open field, next to the river. We don't have time to organize the coliseum. Besides, the fight won't last very long and that would be a total waste." The Kings shouted.

. . . .

"We need to move quickly; the King has announced that we will have the fight in the open field by the river, so we need to set up seats for the King and his cabinet at least." This was the Master of Ceremonies; he was responsible for coordinating all of the events and parties that took place in the palace, or anywhere else the King might fancy to direct him. The fight had already caused a frenzy, and now they were being ordered to move *everything* outside. "What a mess what a mess." The Master of Ceremonies muttered. "How am I supposed to get this done in such a short space of time?" He gasped and dramatically threw the back of his hand against his forehead in dismay. Footman and stable boys and valets and cooks and horseman were flying around the field, in and out of the palace gates, busily trying to follow instructions without colliding with one another.

By the time the King and all his guests made it to the open field, there was a table set up and the royal throne for the King. "Marvelous." Though the King expected nothing less, he was nevertheless impressed with speedy work of his servants. "How very thoughtful of my servants." He thought. He looked over to the Master of Ceremonies who, anxiously awaiting his Sire's approval, looked as though he would faint from the pressure of maintaining his composure. "Well done, Fontaine." The Master of Ceremonies' eyes streamed with tears of joy. "Oh! Thank you, your Royal Highness! Bless you, Bless you!" As Fontaine bowed he indeed fainted, but was barely caught up by his attendants and carried off to a chaise lounge that had been placed nearby.

By now, everyone was out in the open field and ready to watch the fight of the century. It had been a long time since someone actually challenged Ell to a fight. It was the ultimate moment in the recent events of the kingdom, and people from all across the land had come to watch the spectacular display.

"Ladies and gentlemen, the time has come for our main event! I, the King, call for a banquet in honor of everyone present here today. You will all have ale and food after the fight!" Fontaine, who had just recovered and was fanning himself upon the couch, promptly fainted after he perceived that he would now be directing a banquet of such proportions.

. . . .

After Fontaine regained his senses, he began to work masterfully at organizing the festivities. People were running to their posts and dolling out orders left and right, kitchen, banquet, ceremony, with the Master of Ceremonies at the center of it all.

"The King always does this at the last minute. Let us hope the fights last long enough for us to finish the banquet on time." Said the Head Chef. "It is a good thing that we are always prepared. You! Boy! Get on that stove and stir that rue or so'elp me!" He started delegating tasks shouting orders himself. "You! Go and grab the wine from the cellar! And you, set the tables and carry out the appetizers!" It was a complete mad house, though it did seem to have its own chaotic order. "Let us work on the kitchen now, we are going to prepare bread and the meat we were having tonight and combine with more from yesterday and this morning. We cannot fail the King and his guests…People are always hungry after a fight!"

. . . .

As the crowd filtered into the vast field, Shrewder and Faith Woman began to realize just how massive the event truly was.

"This is wild." Remarked Shrewder in almost complete wonder at the size of the sea of people that had formed in just a few hours.

"How does all of this get organized? It's like they *know* what to do, like some hive mind." Commented Faith Woman.

"I dunno, but it's incredible." Replied Shrewder.

The King rose from his throne and strode out to the podium. He raised his hands to call for silence from the crowd, and a silence fell over them massive expanse of onlookers. He paused for a moment, allowing the tension to hang in the hot air. The people knew what was coming, they'd been waiting for what felt like an eternity for someone to challenge their greatest warrior, and now they would see one of the most incredible fights in history.

The whole kingdom seemed to hold its collective breath, until…

"Let the fight begin!" The King bellowed in an unmatched voice of such volume Shrewder thought that thunder had rolled across the land.

Ell began to march into the center of the field, headed right for Shrewder.

"Start with the display of power you showed when fighting Ramu!" Shouted Ell. "I want to see that power."

"As you wish." Said Shrewder. With these words of accent, Shrewder threw his arms out wide and spread his legs on the ground, producing a shockwave of power that stopped Ell's marching.

Chapter 34

"That's it, show me your power." Ell said, shielding his face from the stinging dust that had been kicked up by the wind from Shrewder.

Shrewder became enveloped in red glowing flames that wrapped themselves around him like wisps of sentient power. The fire coiled itself around him tightly like a cocoon, then, after a moment's pause, he exploded from the flames with a thunderclap that leveled the crowd for miles around. As the people recovered, they looked back to see Shrewder completely transformed. Now they beheld him in a suit of crimson armor that shone with it's own otherworldly light. Around his waist was a belt of shimmering silver samite, and at his feet were glistening red sandals lit with flames. The sheer radiative power would've been unbearable for anyone but Ell.

"I now understand why Ramu was no match for your strength. You are incredible." Said Ell.

"And you ain't seen nothing yet." Replied Shrewder.

"Interesting, show me what else you've got, then." Said Ell with a smirk.

"As you wish. I will increase the power of my blows every time I strike you until you can no longer withstand it." Replied Shrewder with seriousness.

Shrewder raced across the field with deadly speed, whirling his sword around to strike Ell. As Ell deftly blocked the blow, with apparent ease, the shockwave that was produced flattened every blade of grass within the vicinity. Shrewder rebounded and immediately lunged for Ell again. This time, he was displaying a red-bronze breastplate which shone brightly in the sun. The second strike, which again Ell blocked, was more powerful, and the force at the edge of Shrewder's blade could've melted steel. Ell seemed to weaken slightly, and bent his knee to the ground under the strain.

"This is a good sign; it has been long time since someone made me bend my knee in a fight." Ell said slyly. In an instant, he rose and threw his first blow. It made contact with Shrewder's shield, sending him flying back. "Excellent, I am glad you managed to block it, otherwise this would've been over much too quickly."

Shrewder skidded in the dust, melting it into glass as he slowed to a stop. He immediately came back on Ell with a ferocious punch to the solar plexus, the first hit that Ell hadn't blocked. A small trickle of blood appeared at the corner of his lips. Ell licked his lips with a smile and counterattacked.

"How's this!?" Ell hammered down upon Shrewder with a sweeping strike that crystalized the sand and shook the ground like an earthquake. The pressure sent Shrewder flying, but he recovered midair and floated gently back down to the ground.

"I assume that you are now fully transformed, yes? This is your full strength?" Ell inquired.

Shrewder merely smiled slightly.

"Let us play for real then." Added Ell.

"Sounds good to me. Honestly I didn't think you'd take it seriously." Shrewder replied with a far away, resonant voice.

The ensuing attacks that the warriors leveled at one another were so immense and overwhelming that people were having trouble keeping up. Amidst the fray, Ell dodged Shrewder's punch and his fist smacked into the ground, creating a fissure that split the field in two. He was bleeding, though he did not know when he'd been hit. "I have to step up my game, otherwise I might lose." He thought to himself.

Shrewder stood and unleashed another burst of power from the depths of his soul.

"I knew you had more in you!" Ell screamed like a wild man, crossing his arms in front of his chest. When he flung his arms wide, he exploded with a fiery white aura, a mirror image of Shrewder.

Shrewder, meanwhile, was walking slowly toward his opponent, flames dripping from his armor and wreathed around his Spartan sandals.

"I'll give you this, boy," said Ell, "no one has ever stood against me in a fight this long."

Shrewder activated the blinding light of his armor, but it did not appear to affect Ell at all. He threw a test punch, and Ell dodged it easily. "I'll need to increase my power. This usually works." He thought.

"trying to trick me, coward!" Ell threw a punch into Shrewder that would've surely killed him had he not blocked with his shield. The impact sent Shrewder to his knees as a terrible cracking echoing across the field. The shield shattered under the strain.

"You are now without a shield." Ell laughed. "How are you going to fight me now? I don't want to kill you just yet."

"I wouldn't worry about it." Said Shrewder, recovering. "I will show you the beauty of my movements…." He flipped up and laned on his feet, visibly shaken. "I need to remember my training."

I believe in my strength, I control my attacks, I endure any strike from my opponent. I show mercy in my fighting style, I portray gentleness and meekness with my blows. I love my fighting style; I find joy and peace in my battle. Shrewder recited these words to himself, but he hadn't realized that Ell was attacking him. As he was thinking to himself, the training had taken over his body. The final dimension of Larey's training had taken hold and become manifest in his every movement.

He was chanting like the words were their own ritual, and in his fighting he was like that of flowing water. But, realizing that he was in a trance like state, he lost his concentration. Ell saw the opportunity, and took it. The strike that he delivered was devastating, and it threw Shrewder clear into the Posin river.

The dust began to clear, and the King stood, shouting to Ell, "Remember the water!"

Nobody could understand what the King was talking about, not even Larey; they were all dumbstruck with the display of power in the fight.

Ell nodded and leapt across the whole filed in one bound. As he splashed into the water to continue the fight, he threw a powerful attack at the floating warrior. He noticed in an instant that Shrewder made no effort to block or evade, and he remembered what his father said about the power of the water.

"What is happening to me? I don't feel any power left. I feel that I cannot continue this fight." Thought Shrewder helplessly. Ell saw the confusion in *Shrewder*'s eyes, and he said,

"My friend, this is between you and me; I want no mysterious spell or power to interfere. Let us step out of the river if you want to continue fighting."

"I am fine. I can continue." He replied.

"No," Ell insisted, "you are not understanding me. One of the secret powers of Posin river is that if a human or mortal enters its domain, he or she will become powerless."

"I see," replied Shrewder, "any other fighter would have taken advantage of this situation, but you instead have shown me mercy and honesty."

"Don't get me wrong. I'm still going to beat you, I just don't need any tricks to defeat my opponents; I am one of the strongest in all Nede Land, it would be a shame to win using tricks and dirty games." Concluded Ell, reaching out to pull Shrewder from the river by the hand.

Just the two of them were in the river and no one was able to hear their conversation. The King was getting anxious because he saw them coming out of the water. He yelled to Ell,

"What are you doing? Remember what we discussed!" Ell did not pay attention to the King, and continued to assist Shrewder. The crowd was confused by this, and did not know how to react.

"I feel frustrated, it looks like my father does not trust my power and strength. To even *suggest* such a dirty trick to win a fight…makes me sick. I am Ell of Babul Ell Kingdom and there is no one who can defeat me." He thought to himself.

When Shrewder stepped out of the water, he felt his power and energy coming back to his body like a stream of electricity through his veins.

He jumped up into the air and his newly recovered power radiated from him and completely evaporated the water from his body. He opened his arms with such force that his armor cracked and fell away and clanged on the hard ground, revealing his body in its fullest splendor. The number two shone brightly on his right upper chest and was visible to everyone. His muscles were an incredible sight to behold, rippling and coursing with unmatched power.

When Ell approached, he said to Shrewder, "Are you ready to resume the fight?"

"I have never been more ready." He replied.

Ell looked down at Shrewder's chest. "Out of curiosity, what does the number on your chest means?"

 I will share with you since you have shown me kindness. This is the representation of my strength, or rank. There is only one stronger than me and he is not coming to this kingdom. He should be now fighting and beating some fighters in this world."

"Interesting! I would love to meet that warrior someday." Beamed Ell.

"Sadly, you will not have the opportunity to see another day." Added Shrewder, with resolute conviction.

Shrewder had now begun to truly master his training, using the elements he learned from the great Larey. He shook his body in a sign to continue the battle.

"Are you sure you want to continue without your armor?"

"Don't worry about it, there is a secret that I have just discovered, and the armor can be of no more use to me." The armor, in fact, was nowhere to be seen, it had completely vanished.

Chapter 35

"What are you doing Shrewder? Why you are not transformed and wearing your armor?" Inquired Faith Woman, speaking to him in her mind.

"It is ok, I have discovered the real secret behind the armor. It looks like we never learned to use it properly, we never understood our armor, but today I have come to understand it and I can fully use the power of the armor."

"The breastplate of righteousness, the feet with the gospel of peace, the shield of faith, the helmet of salvation. Do you understand it now, Faith Woman? Our armor is not complete, that is one of the reasons why we came to this kingdom, and we still need the Sword of the Spirit for the armor's potential to be fully unlocked. And, more importantly, the visible armor was just an ornament, because the real armor is engraved on our souls. My body is my armor now; a fully equipped mind and soul are my weapons. Do not worry, I will be fine, even though I am not yet complete."

. . . .

"Coming at you!" Shouted Ell, manifesting incredible strength and speed. Shrewder readied himself and was met with strike after strike, blow after blow, but to no effect. No blood, no bruises, no scratches could be seen.

"But how is he blocking my blows?" Wondered Ell. "He is using his own body as a shield, but he is not bleeding. What is going on? I am now using 70 percent of my strength and he is able to keep up with me." In that instant, Shrewder caught Ell's fist in his hand, turned it aside and winked. A massive build up of energy emerged from Shrewder, causing Ell to increase his effort and shake of Shrewder's grip. Shrewder, though only at 90 percent of his true strength, decided to unleash everything he was capable of summon without the Sword, and what an immense display.

His power was overwhelming. It was so strong that King Babul Ell felt the desire to stand up and fight. "I have been looking for a fight like that one!" He was exhilarated. "How jealous I am today of my son. I had no idea this guy had such strength. Where is it coming from?" Wondered the King.

Ell was now facing a completely new warrior. The red that had glimmered in his armor was now coming out of his body; he was barefoot but still the flames were at his feet as before.

"His power is immense. This guy is stronger than me at the moment." Ell was thinking that he needed to change something fast when, suddenly, he felt a blow in his stomach so intense it made him curl up and fall over, blood gushing from his right arm. "I have to increase my strength or next time it is not going to be my right arm but my head that caves in." Thought Ell. "I cannot believe that I have to use almost my full strength on this guy."

"Where did you learn to fight like this?" Asked Ell.

"Don't worry, I prefer to show you." Replied Shrewder. He burst into a roil of flames and rushed Ell, aiming to finish the fight. But Ell unleashed a firestorm of power and gained the upper hand, countering Shrewder's blow and throwing him into the dirt, hard. Shrewder looked down and winced in pain as he realized he was bleeding from the left leg. He slammed his fists into the ground, generating an immense propelling force that sent him hurling in Ell's direction. As he flew through the air, he performed a somersault kick that struck Ell on the shoulder, downing him in an explosion of dust and mud.

"What an incredible battle." Whispered Larey. "I never thought Shrewder's potential could be so high, reaching such devastating heights, but something is still missing." He turned his inward eye upon the field to investigate what he felt coming from his pupil. "It looks like he has not completely grasped the training."

Meanwhile, Faith Woman, who had been watching the fight intently, was almost completely engrossed in thought. "Shrewder, when did you become so strong? I never thought I would see you become this strong; I could not even imagine that something like this was possible. I have a very long way to go before I catch up with you. Keep up the fight and hang on, I will catch up with you someday." She thought.

"Wow! He is so strong; he is keeping up with the great Ell. That warrior has hurt Ell. Who is he? Is he going to defeat our Prince?" Fontaine exclaimed.

"Don't worry, Ell has never lost a battle and he isn't about to start now, I can tell you." Replied one of the soldiers standing guard next to him.

"I never thought I could see this day, the day when the power of this kingdom would be challenged and matched; but he is not the one, not quite. There is another one greater than he and when he comes, he will conquer. He will not have mercy on us. This is the first sign that the ultimate warrior is about to come to Nede Land." Thought an old man watching the fight from a distance in the bushes.

. . . .

Both warriors were injured now, and both were trying desperately to finish the fight. Breathing heavily and perspiring profusely, they jumped up into the air at the same time and appeared to vanish. Nothing but the ripples in the air and the shockwaves from their mighty blows could be seen, and only the clash of swords and the thunderclaps from their fists striking one another could be heard. This no longer appeared to be a fight between mortals, but rather a fight between celestial beings.

In this nebula of unmatched strength that the fighters had created around them, as if time-locked in a bubble of ferocious power, only they could perceive one another. Ell shouted above the din of roar of the whirlwind, "The battle will be over with my next move, Shrewder! Are you prepared to meet your god?!"

Shrewder replied, "I should ask you the same!" In that definitive moment, all the world seemed to fade from their periphery; the color and vividity of the field and the people and the flowing water melted away, and for an instant, all that remained were the two rivals and the tempest of their power. An eternity passed before the two struck each other with their swords, and the force that was generated between them shattered the blades and thrust the men out of the vortex, stranding them in mid air before the whole kingdom. The two fell into the river, gasping and exhausted, with an enormous splash.

Still submerged, Shrewder thought, "Not again, not again, please." His power was being drained away with each passing second. They both surfaced and emerged from the water, struggling to make it to shore.

Ell gasped and said, "This has been enough exercise for today. Should we decide to finish the fight? We will need new swords and you will surely die." He was panting and sucking in huge mouthfuls of air like a marathon runner who had reached the end of the race.

He continued. "Up till now, you have forced me to use 85 percent of my strength; if I use my full strength, you will die…and…you are a worthy opponent. But I can see that you cannot increase your power anymore, you've reached your limit."

Shrewder replied. "I felt like you still had more power hidden in you and you were still not fighting at full capacity. I agree with you, we can call it a draw for now. But if I call it a draw, I will not get any reward, will I?"

"You are the best I've ever fought," Ell reached over and grabbed Shrewder's shoulder in an embrace, "I will make sure you get at least one of the rewards, you have my word."

"Ladies and gentlemen, and your Majesty the King! The fight is over!" Called Ell. The people were dumbstruck. They started mumbling and gasping.

"But who is the winner?" They were thinking.

"We have decided to call it a draw! Since my rival has shown incredible strength, I have given my word that he can have access to the Secret Chamber treasures and withdraw one item worthy of his bravery and courage! *That* is my word and my vow. I Prince Ell of Babul Ell Kingdom has given my word, and my word is my bond."

The King stood as if to speak, yet he only reaffirmed the Prince's words by saying, "Prince Ell has spoken, and it shall be so. Let us all enjoy the feast!"

The feast was unlike anything that Shrewder or Faith Woman had ever experienced. They were welcomed and treated with such dignity and respect, that they could hardly speak. Shrewder was hoisted on high and given a seat of honor near the King. His worn body was tended to and he was smoothed over with sweet smelling oils and perfumes. He was given the first selection of all the food and drink, and his heart's desires were met immediately.

Chapter 36

Faith Woman and Shrewder were now like part of the kingdom, they did not need to stay hidden from the people any longer; they were acknowledged as strong and brave which are among the most important qualities in Babul Ell Kingdom.

"It looks like I don't have to babysit you anymore." Said Larey coming up from behind them to congratulate his pupils. "You have made me proud and you have shown incredible power. I know that you were not at your full strength, it seemed to me that there is still something missing in your fighting style." Added Larey in a low voice. "But I am eager to see you develop that little bit you are missing. You could surely defeat anyone in the kingdom…except me." He smiled and the three of them laughed heartily.

"I have failed in my goal; I did not expect a draw. I was expecting something more dramatic, a defeat perhaps. I must find a way to bring justice to the King and justify my cause for the sake of my love. It hurts so much not to have you with me, darling. I have failed you this time, but it will not happen again." Thought Larey while immersed in the depth of his mind, amid the screams and cheers of the party.

"You were saying something? It looks like I lost you for a second, buddy! Where did you go this time?" Asked Shrewder in a sign of concern. It was not the first time Larey had become lost in his thoughts for a second or two. "I know you must have felt disappointed with the fight, I did my best, but Ell is too strong and as you said, I am really missing the key factor that would allow me to complete my power. I am yet to figure out how to get it." Shrewder hung his head in sadness.

"It is not the time to worry about the past, you were great!" Reassured Larey. "You are the first one to stand up and come out alive after fighting a battle against Ell. It is not for nothing that he is considered one of the strongest in the kingdom and maybe in all Nede Land." Shrewder lightened a bit as he heard this. "Come, let us now attend to your wounds. I think you must be hungry and thirsty, you have earned the privilege of eating and drinking with the people, the both of you!" Said Larey with genuine pride for his students.

The night went well, they were all enjoying themselves and experiencing the oneness of the people of this great land. They felt like they were part of the kingdom from the warmth and kindness from everyone present. But even more, they felt that the whole land was rejoicing and celebrating with them.

"You almost beat our Prince!" Some said. "But *almost* is not a win!" Some laughed, but in good humor. "The prince! Our prince! The strongest!" The cheers were loud and exuberant.

"Prince Ell is still undefeated and will stay that way forever!" One shouted. "Prince Ell, drink with us! We want to drink with our hero!" Ell sat down with his people in celebration.

Ell knew somewhere deep in his heart that there was someone almost as strong as he was; he could even *surpass* him one day. "How can it be that a mere human is that strong? If that was him without the Holy Relics my father told me about, I cannot imagine how strong and formidable he'll become if he manages to get the Secret Treasures. Well, at least I helped a little by granting him one. Am I contributing to my own destruction? Nah! I will stop thinking nonsense and enjoy the company of my people!" Thought Ell, shrugging off the pangs of future warnings.

. . . .

Three days later, the King summoned Faith Woman and Shrewder to the presence of Ell. It was time to enter the Secret Chamber of treasures and retrieve his reward for fighting so bravely and fearlessly.

"I am the guardian and I will fulfill my promise. You will enter the Chamber and you will be able to choose one treasure only. If you are able to retrieve it, you will be able to take it with you.

"That "if" sounds like problem, but I am up to the task." Replied Shrewder. As they approached the Chamber. Shrewder could hear voices calling him from within. "Faith Woman, can you hear the voices calling from within the chamber?" He said, perplexedly.

"No, I don't hear anything." She replied, straining her ears.

"That is weird, because I can hear voices calling me. But it is ok, never mind." As they got closer the voices grew louder, but only Shrewder was able to hear them.

"I must warn you, the power hidden here is not supposed to leave this Chamber," Warned King Babul Ell, "but I will abide the word of my son."

Shrewder and Faith Woman proceeded with caution.

As soon as they opened the main door to the Secret Chamber, they felt like the earth was shaking and the four pillars vibrating. They could hear something moving within, and at this point, Ell said,

"You can select your Holy Relic from one of these two pillars and you will need to retrieve it yourself."

Ell made sure that they were encouraged to choose from the group of *Gifts* and not from the most powerful group of all, the *Fruits*. On each pillar there was an inscription that described the power contained within. The first one read "*Discernment*" and the second read "*Miracles*."

When Shrewder reached out to choose, suddenly, the pillar containing the power of Discernment cracked, and they could see through the fissure that something was flickering inside. It was a brilliantly shining broadsword. Shrewder could hear it saying, "*You have come for me, and I am going with you.*" And in that moment, the sword broke through the icy stone of the pillar and flew directly into Shrewder's right hand.

"Look!" Faith Woman shouted. The other pillars began to shake as well, but Shrewder still could not understand what the voices were saying. A resonance between the pillars began to arise, like a giant tuning fork reverberating through the entire chamber. Each of the three pillars began to quake and tremble terribly, until the pitch reached such a volume that all within began to cover their ears in pain.

"What's happening, father?" Shouted Ell.

"I do not know! This…this has never happened before!" Suddenly, the easternmost pillar split in two, then the southern pillar followed immediately after and a bright light spilled out from inside them. Finally, just before the group could stand it no longer, the west pillar shattered into a million shards. The group began to recover, and as they looked up, they beheld the fading light within the pillars, and as it faded, they perceived a brilliant and handsome sword nestled in the middle of each.

"What..." Before Shrewder could finish his sentence, one of the swords leapt from the stony cradle and flew straight for his left hand. One other sword stirred and bolted from its pillar as well. King Babul Ell, however, being as strong as he is, caught the sword with one hand. The fourth sword was breaking through as well, but Ell managed to grab it and stop it from breaking through.

King Babul Ell immediately Spokane an incantation of some sort, they could not understand, but it had the effect of sealing the three remaining pillars, locking the three most powerful swords back in place.

"I am here too, and none of these swords came to me. They were rejecting me...why is that?" Thought Faith Woman to herself,

"Why did the swords break through and go to that man? Who is that man that that these three powerful weapons are calling for him?" Thought king Babul Ell.

. . . .

"You may enjoy one more day in the kingdom; tomorrow Larey will open the gate and escort you back to your world." Said king Babul Ell with a look of astonishment and fear on his noble face.

Dear Reader,

I hope you enjoyed the first books in the series: *The Hero Within: Awareness, The Hero Within: Power & The Hero Within – Nede Land 1*.

I have to tell you, I really love this hero story. Many readers wrote me asking, "What's next for our Hero?" Well, be sure to stay tuned because the saga of publishing Christian Fiction isn't quite over. Our Hero will be back in book four. Will he have more power? I sure hope so.

When I wrote *The Hero Within: Nede Land 2;* I got many letters from fans thanking me for the books. Some had opinions adventures, while others simply rooted for Ell.

As an author, I love feedback. Candidly, you're the reason I will explore the Hero's future. So tell me what you liked, what you loved, even what you hated. You can write me at comments@christianhero.org and visit me on the web at www.christianhero.org.

Finally, I need to ask a favor. If you're so inclined, I'd love a review of *The Hero Within: Nede Land 2*. Loved it, hated it—I'd just enjoy your feedback.

Reviews can be tough to come by these days, and you, the reader have the power to make or break a book. If you have the time, ***here's a link to my author page, along with all my books on Amazon: http://amzn.to/19p3dNx***

Thank you so much for reading *The Hero Within: Nede Land 2* and for spending time with me.

In gratitude,

Dr. Yeral E. Ogando

Dr. Yeral E. Ogando comes from a very humble origin and continues to be a humble servant of our Lord Almighty; understanding that we are nothing but vessels and the Lord who called us, also sends us to do His work, not our work. *Luke 17:10 "So likewise ye, when ye shall have done all those things which are commanded you, say, We are unprofitable servants: we have done that which*

was our duty to do."

Mr. Ogando was born in the Caribbean, Dominican Republic. He is the beloved father of two beautiful girls "Yeiris & Tiffany" and three handsome boys "Bennett, Ethan & Nathan"

Jesus brought him to His feet at the age of 16-17. Since then, he has served as Co-pastor, pastor, Bible School teacher, youth counselor, and church planter.

Fluent in several languages Mr. Ogando is the Creator and owner of an Online Translation Ministry operating since 2007; with Native Christian translators in more than 25 countries and translating into more than 250 languages. (www.christian-translation.com),

The most exciting thing about his Translation Ministry is that thousands of people are receiving the Word of God in their native language on a daily basis and hundreds of ministries are able to reach the world through the work of Christian-Translation.com along with his network of websites in different languages related to Christian Translation and Christian Services.

He's earned several degrees among them: Master of Arts in Theological Studies, Master of Arts in Languages and Linguistics and Doctor of Philosophy in Theology.

I would like you to share with me your impression and / or ideas after reading my books. Feel free to email them to me at comments@christianhero.org. It would be my honor to hear your thoughts about *The Hero Within Saga.*

1. What part of the story did you like the most?

2. What part of the story did you like the least?

3. Which one was your favorite character and why?

4. What have you learned after reading the series?

5. *There is a secret message behind most of the names, but only by using your imagination you will decode them.* Which ones were you able to decode?

6. Which ones were the hardest to decode?

7. What is your general impression on the books?

8. What do you expect to happen next and what would you like to happen? *I will surely take your ideas into consideration and if they are good enough, I will definitely mention your name when taking them into considerations.*

9. Finally, Make sure to check the Manga version at www.christianhero.org

By completing this challenge properly, you are entering *The Hero Within Challenge.* We will select 10 winners with different prizes. Make sure to state that you want to participate in *The Hero Within Challenge* when sending your feedback form.